W9-CJN-890

$3.95

Runaway Horse

TRANSLATED BY

LEILA VENNEWITZ

RUNAWAY

HORSE

A NOVEL BY *Martin Walser*

An Owl Book

HENRY HOLT AND COMPANY   NEW YORK

Copyright © 1978 by Suhrkamp Verlag Frankfurt am Main
Translation copyright © 1980 by Martin Walser and Leila
Vennewitz
All rights reserved, including the right to reproduce this book
or portions thereof in any form.
Published by Henry Holt and Company, Inc.,
521 Fifth Avenue, New York, New York 10175.
Distributed in Canada by Fitzhenry & Whiteside Limited,
195 Allstate Parkway, Markham, Ontario L3R 4T8.
Originally published in Germany under the title Ein
Fliehendes Pferd.

Library of Congress Cataloging-in-Publication Data
Walser, Martin, 1927–
Runaway horse.
"An Owl book."
Translation of Ein Fliehendes Pferd.
I. Title.
PZ4.W222Ru [PT2685.A48]   833'.9'14   79-22749
ISBN: 0-8050-0359-2 (pbk.)

First published in hardcover in the United States by Holt,
Rinehart and Winston in 1980.
First Owl Book Edition—1987
Printed in the United States of America
10 9 8 7 6 5 4 3 2 1

ISBN 0-8050-0359-2

Translator's Acknowledgment

William Vennewitz, my husband,
has given me unstinting assistance
and advice throughout this
translation, and I am deeply
grateful to him.

Leila Vennewitz

FOR FRANZISKA

"From time to time one comes across novellas in which certain persons expound opposing philosophies. A preferred ending is for one of these persons to convince the other. Thus, instead of the philosophy having to speak for itself, the reader is favored with the historical result that the other person has been convinced. I regard it as a blessing that in this respect these papers afford no enlightenment."

—Sören Kierkegaard, *Either/Or*

Runaway Horse

1 ᾧ Suddenly Sabina pushed her way out of the tide of tourists surging along the promenade and headed for a little table that was still unoccupied. Helmut had the feeling that the chairs in this café were too small for him, but Sabina had already sat down. Nor would he ever have chosen one in the front row. Sitting that close to the crowds moving past in both directions, you really couldn't see a thing. He would have chosen a spot as close to the building as possible. Otto had also sat down. At Sabina's feet. But he was still gazing up at Helmut as if to say that, as long as Helmut was not yet seated, he regarded his own posture as temporary.

Sabina promptly ordered coffee, crossed one leg over the other, and regarded the sluggish back-and-forth on the lakeside promenade with an expression of enjoyment intended solely for Helmut's benefit. He switched his gaze back to the people strolling too closely past. There was little enough to see. But of that little, too much. He felt a kind of hopeless craving for those brightly, lightly clad, suntanned figures. They looked more attractive here than back home in Stuttgart. He did not feel the same way about himself. He felt ridiculous in light-colored pants. When he wasn't wearing a jacket, the most noticeable thing about him was probably his stomach. After a week he wouldn't

1

mind. But on the third day he still did, just as he minded his hideous sunburned skin. Another week, and Sabina and he would be tanned too. As for Sabina, all the sun had achieved so far was to puff up every little wrinkle, every tiny flaw in her skin. Sabina looked grotesque. Particularly now, as she gazed delightedly at the passersby. He placed his hand on her forearm. Why on earth did they have to sit here looking at this thrusting tangle of arms and legs and breasts? What's more, in their vacation apartment it would be much cooler by now than on this concrete, treeless promenade. And every second passerby wafted such an air of adventure under one's nose that watching them turned into swiftly mounting unhappiness. They were all younger. How pleasant it would be now behind the straight iron bars of their vacation apartment windows. They had been here three days, and for three evenings he had had to follow Sabina into town. Each time to this promenade. She found people-watching interesting. So it was. But intolerable.

He had planned to read Kierkegaard's diaries and had brought along all five volumes. And may the Lord have mercy on you, Sabina, if he only gets through four. He hadn't the faintest idea what Kierkegaard had entered in his diaries. Unimaginable that Kierkegaard could have jotted down anything private. He yearned to get closer to Kierkegaard. Perhaps he was only yearning so that he could be disappointed. He visualized those many hours of daily disappointment over Kierkegaard's diaries as something enjoyable. Like a rainy day on vacation. If these diaries permitted no proximity, as he feared (and still more hoped), his yearning to get closer to this man would increase. A diary devoid of anything private: what could be more fascinating? He must tell Sabina that, starting tomorrow, he would be spending all his evenings in the apartment. He could have trembled with indignation! Sitting here on this inadequate chair, staring at people, while in the apartment he . . .

He did not want to take Kierkegaard down to the lake. That was something he had done as a boy of fifteen. He had read *Zarathustra* while lying on his stomach. Snob that he was, he had read the French translation. *Ainsi parlait Zarathustra.*

Sabina's enjoyment of the passing throng had meanwhile produced a smile that remained fixed. He felt embarrassed for Sabina's smile. He touched her arm. They should probably be conversing. An aging couple sitting mutely on café chairs and observing such a lively scene is an odd sight. Or a pathetic one. Especially when the woman is still wearing that long-defunct smile. Helmut did not like people around them to have ideas about himself and Sabina that were accurate. Never mind what people thought about them both as long as it was wrong. To succeed in promoting mistaken conclusions always made him feel good. Incognito: that was his dearest image. In Stuttgart he had to accept the fact that knowledge about him was increasing among neighbors and at school—among his fellow teachers as well as his students. The nickname "Kiwi" had stuck to him. This showed him that he had been perceived, unmasked, and tagged with almost inimitable accuracy. Whenever, in school or in his neighborhood, he saw evidence of being recognized for what he was, of familiarity with at-

tributes to which he had never admitted, he wanted
to escape. To run away, away, away. They made use
of a knowledge about him whose accuracy he had
not conceded. Made use of it to deal with him.
To subordinate him. To make him perform. They
knew how to manipulate him. And the more
they knew how to manipulate him, the greater
became his longing to be once again unrecognized.
As long as someone knew nothing about him, all
things were possible. Unfortunately he had not always fully realized that, which was why he had not
prevented those familiarities. Now all that was left
to him was escape. Once or twice a year. His vacation, in fact. On vacation he would try out faces and
manners that seemed to him appropriate for shield-
ing his true person from the eyes of the world. To
be inaccessible, that became his dream. And he
found it difficult not to allow the slender, pointed,
steep-sided rocky fortress to become a permanent
image. A kind of super-Neuschwanstein seemed to
be burning itself into his imagination. And forests.
Always he saw forests. Saw himself trotting through
forests. Without moving he would trot along, penetrating farther and farther into the forest which,
fortunately, never ended. Forests without end, that
must be perfection.

Had he in fact really wanted to become a
teacher? Does anyone really want to become anything? Might this longing to remain unrecognized
harbor the wish to be younger? On taking up his
first post he had published a short paragraph in the
school newspaper that he still knew by heart. When
he said the lines over to himself, he grinned as if he
had to listen to a joke that offended his sense of
decency:

A Teacher's Enthusiasm

I refer to a circumscribed subject which the teacher does not fully master but which he presents with the utmost vigor. The students will be better informed on the subject itself from other quarters. But in listening to the persistent words of this teacher they have learned something of which they were not aware. His absurdity is a lesson that will last them a lifetime. They will look back on it reverently. The deeper the teacher fades into the past, the more exalted will the students' reverence become.

Probably he was grinning because of the scruples that prevented him from simply suppressing such thoughts.

How pleasant it was to arrive at the Zürns' house, where for the past eleven years they had occupied the vacation apartment for four weeks; to be aware of automatically producing the role that one acted here.

His behavior toward Mrs. Zürn had taken shape during their first stay eleven years ago and could subsequently be deemed fixed. She regarded him as cheerful, talkative, in need of a rest, fond of flowers, devoted to animals, crazy about children, with a heart of gold. . . .

He had not invented the vacation role that Mrs. Zürn expected of him. All he had done was adjust his behavior to accord with his notion of what Mrs. Zürn liked best. The result had agreeably little to do with him. True, the smile that Mrs. Zürn produced as soon as he and Sabina appeared might also have nothing to do with her. So much the better. In eleven years her husband had not had a single real conversation with him. With Sabina, yes. He and this Dr. Zürn continued to pass each other as two mysteries of equal status. He had already told Sabina that he found this Dr. Zürn more likable than anyone else. Didn't they even resemble each other? Round shoulders, round stomach. And heavyset. In the slightly exaggerated courtesy with which they were treated by the Zürns, Helmut perceived the degree of reserve that was most agreeable to him. He did not wish to know what kind of a doctor Dr. Zürn was, or why the Zürns were still renting out an apartment in their beautiful lakeside home, any more than the Zürns wished to know from them why in eleven years no other vacation spot had suggested itself to them. The most splendid thing about this vacation relationship was its annually increasing but totally detached familiarity. They had never progressed beyond the basis that eleven years ago both the Zürns and they had owned a young spaniel. Now the Zürns as well as they themselves owned an old spaniel. In spite of all this, he could think of no one with whom he felt more at ease than Dr. and Mrs. Zürn. Toward their four daughters, on the other hand, he maintained the same reserve as toward the rest of humanity. Oh, if only they could be out there now at the Zürns'!

Sabina said: "You're not getting impatient, are you?" She was not looking at him as she spoke. Anyone watching her from a distance would have deduced from her expression that she had said to her husband: Sitting here with you is just fabulous. He said: "Impatient? Whatever makes you think that?" She said: "Are you hungry?" "Hungry," he said in a solemn, melodramatic tone. "Shall we go?" she asked. "Back to the apartment," he said.

"No, to have supper somewhere," she said. "Are you hungry?" he asked. "We shouldn't have eaten all that cake after lunch," she said. "You baked it," he said. "I know," she said guiltily. "If only you wouldn't make such good cakes," he said gloomily.

There's no salvation anyway, he thought. He had no idea why he thought it. Save mankind, he told himself. Go ahead and save it. Maybe Sabina can enjoy this people-watching. He didn't think so. She would have to be quite different from him. But she isn't. They have affected each other. They now have an uncanny resemblance to each other. Just look at her smile. Probably, without being aware of it, you are at this moment wearing exactly the same precipitous smile. Anyone seeing you like this is bound to take you for twins. And just then Sabina said: "I think we both already have spaniel faces." This happened over and over again: She would make a remark that was like an answer to what he happened at that very moment to be thinking. On this occasion it annoyed him. Shut up, he thought, and immediately felt acutely embarrassed at having been so harsh with Sabina in his thoughts. "Don't fight so hard," Sabina said, placing her hand on his. He withdrew his hand and stroked Otto, saying: "He's insulted, and no wonder, because you said we resembled him, whereas you're the only one who resembles him, I don't at all." "Separatist," she said. "Are you having a good time here?" he asked. "I could watch people forever," she said. "I couldn't," he said. "Too bad," she said. "I'm leaving now," he said furiously. "Just one more minute," she said. "By all means," he said, and looked at his watch.

7

2 ❧ *Suddenly a slight,* trim young man was standing by their table. Wearing blue jeans. A blue shirt, open down to his rawhide belt, which was decorated with poker-work symbols. And beside him a girl divided into two distinct halves by the seam of her jeans. Just as she, wherever one looked, was all soft and round, he was all vertical, athletic, without an ounce of spare flesh. On his deeply tanned chest grew only a few golden hairs, but from his head sprang a blazing blond mop. Probably one of his former students, thought Helmut. Unfortunately it happens all the time, former students coming up and speaking to you. And more often than not it's the ones who did their utmost to make your job as a teacher unbearable. The very ones who used to make your life thoroughly miserable now suddenly stand there in front of you, grinning, holding out their hands, introducing some wild female or some stunning girl like this one; maybe even a few merrily shrieking kids who paw you with sticky fingers; then they proceed to rattle off their fantastic life stories and confess their remorse, insisting that it took them years to realize what a *super* teacher you had been. . . . These sentimental gushings from his former tormentors aroused only revulsion and disgust in him. While they were talking, he would keep his eyes fixed on the toes of their shoes or their feet. Just as he did in school. Hence the nickname "Kiwi." It must have been the girls who had induced this posture of head and body in him. With their pitiless blouses and pants. On one occasion his power of dissimulation had deserted him: he had reached out; fortunately the girl in question had regarded it as inadvertent.

No, the man in blue with the blaze of golden hair, with such white eyeballs and such white teeth and his bare feet and beautiful pristine toes, was no student, he was Klaus Buch. And Klaus Buch refused to believe that his classmate and boyhood pal and fellow student Helmut did not recognize him. Helmut could merely reiterate his apologies. His memory for faces and names was professionally exhausted, he claimed; he had had to remember far too many faces and names. Klaus Buch . . .—he lied his way along—. . . of course, now both the name and the face began to seem familiar. And so that's Sabina, Helmut's wife. And this is Helene, known as Hella, Klaus's wife. As he shook hands with Hella, he sensed that Klaus expected a compliment. This woman was like a trophy. At least Helmut should now have told his former friend Klaus how puzzled he, Helmut, was because Klaus looked more like a student of Helmut's. Although now forced grudgingly to admit having had a friend whose name was Klaus Buch and who had looked like the young man confronting him, he was totally unable to relate this person to the Klaus Buch who was gradually surfacing in his memory, simply because by now *his* Klaus Buch must also be forty-six, whereas the man confronting him must surely be closer to twenty-six. Like his girl. Above all *because* of his girl. Helmut said nothing of all this. No compliments. That'll get you. He looked down at their feet. Her toes, too, lay straight and snugly side by side. The two were talking away. Still talking, they sat down. Seated, they went on talking. Helmut thought of Kierkegaard's diaries. Sabina supplied all the information required by Hella's and Klaus's nonstop talking. Helmut nodded. Suddenly Klaus Buch jumped up with a shriek and waved one hand about as if it had been burned or pierced by a bullet. Helmut and Sabina were baffled. Fortunately Helene Buch laughed. After regaining control of himself, Klaus Buch looked carefully under the table. "Is that animal yours?" he asked. "But he has never yet bitten anyone," said Sabina. Hella said: "With his paranoia about dogs, the slightest touch is enough to set off a trauma." Sabina said: "Down, Otto." She apologized profusely to Klaus Buch and promised to keep an eye on Otto.

Well, would you believe it, for three years they've also been coming here for their vacation. And staying out at Maurach. "That's less than a mile from where we are," said Sabina. They, Sabina and Helmut, had been staying out that way for the past eleven years. They, Hella and Klaus, were fed up with the Mediterranean. What a joke, for three years they had been spending their vacations side by side and had never bumped into each other. Well, if that isn't a joke, Helmut! Say, Helmut, what do you say to that? Sure, he also thinks it's a joke. Hella and Klaus go sailing a lot. Sabina and Helmut prefer to laze around by the water, or just sit around. It sounded as if she were complaining to Klaus Buch about Helmut. Helmut nodded. He knew Sabina wasn't really complaining. It happened to suit her to pretend that she was. Perhaps it was a kind of compliment directed at Klaus Buch.

She became all enthusiastic about the enthusiasm which this meeting had aroused in Klaus Buch. That he should be so pleased to have met her husband again apparently made her feel good. She looked at Klaus Buch in a kind of bliss. As if she had been waiting for him for a long time and was now hanging on his every word. This Klaus Buch couldn't stop enthusing about his boyhood friend Helmut. Had read *Zarathustra* at fourteen. Way ahead of all of them. Puberty with a crown of thorns. A sort of ingrown single-mindedness. From the very beginning. Right? Klaus Buch phrased his sentences in such a way that, in agreeing or disagreeing, one merely agreed or disagreed with his phrasing, not with the content. Helmut had always been the prophet in suspenders, hadn't he! Saint Frantic in person! Simply inflamed. Barefoot and inflamed, that's the only way he knew his Helmut. Quite often the inflammation had switched from the mental to the physical. Once a month, for four or five days, all one could do was look up at the windows of the room where—and behind horrible russet drapes at that—Helmut was letting his inflammation burn itself out. Helmut interrupted him. He wanted to get away from here. By this time other people must be listening in. Besides, he felt that Klaus Buch's wife must be bored listening to these phrases that didn't in any way concern her. But he wasn't going to let them escape, said Klaus Buch. He herewith invited the Halms to dinner and wasn't going to listen to any kind of refusal.

This fellow really does remember my name. After about . . . Helmut stood up and as casually as possible asked when they had last met. "You don't remember?" cried Klaus Buch. He refused to believe it. It was exactly twenty-three years, almost to the day. He, Klaus Buch, had then left Tübingen after getting himself that post at Edinburgh. After the farewell dinner Helmut had insisted—remember?—that Klaus take a dip in the fountain on the market square. Accustomed to doing whatever Helmut said, he did as he was told. Surely Helmut couldn't have forgotten that? Helmut pretended to recollect every detail of all that Klaus Buch was scooping up with such largesse as if out of a puppeteer's box. But he remembered nothing. If the fellow hadn't mentioned *Zarathustra* and the frequent attacks of tonsillitis, it might have been a case of mistaken identity. Even the russet drapes seemed stagy. Had they had russet drapes at home? And what do horrible drapes look like? On no account must he let on what a total stranger this Klaus Buch seemed to him. True, in the darkest corner of his memory something was nibbling away that might be the name of this person. And this blondness, this nimble, trim elegance, this laugh that seemed to ring out for the benefit of his teeth . . . that might have been. That jutting jaw, those perfect teeth and almost obscenely mobile lips, they might have been there in his youth. But then again they might not. On the other hand, the fellow knew so much about mutual friends which Helmut recognized that a mistake was out of the question.

Perhaps Helmut had erased this Klaus Buch from his memory. Hadn't he at one time envied someone who had obtained a lectureship at Edinburgh? He believed he had. And there had been a young Klaus who seemed to have everything. So this was the fellow. That house with windows as tall as church windows, with stained glass, that had

12

been their house; behind dark trees; somber. He had never been inside. He had been afraid. Only once, when he knew they were all away at the North Sea, had he climbed over the wall and, from behind the bushes, studied the garden and that tall house. Didn't it have a bay window that with the aid of a separate pointed roof seemed to be trying to turn into a turret? Suddenly he had had to bolt. In terror.

"Didn't you have a bike with balloon tires?" Helmut asked. "Ri-ight!" cried Klaus Buch. "At last! Jesus, I was beginning to wonder whether you didn't want to know me!"

Klaus said he would take them to the Hecht for dinner. "With the greatest of pleasure," said Helmut.

3 ✦ *It began to dawn* on Helmut that by this time Klaus Buch had run out of witnesses for certain cherished years of his life. And these were the very years he apparently wished to preserve intact. In order to revive the past, he needed a partner who, at least by nods and looks, would confirm that it had been thus and so. Without this partner he would be quite unable to talk about those days. Helmut realized that it was a case of the war-buddy syndrome. Personally, he lacked this fanatical desire to resurrect bygone days. Every memory of the past depressed him. He felt a kind of loathing when he considered how much past history had already accumulated in him. Put the lid on it. Keep it closed. Don't let any oxygen get at it or it would start to ferment. Klaus Buch was different. When he found a thread, he wanted all the others connected with it. He wouldn't give up until he felt sure of having the entire fabric of an afternoon twenty-five years ago once more before his eyes. Or at least the design. Or the colors. Or at least the idea. Generally speaking, however, this Klaus Buch was so well informed about past happenings that Helmut was staggered. According to him, there had been boxes of geraniums around the edge of that fountain and before Klaus Buch had been able to take the dip ordered by Helmut they had removed two of them. The girl studying theology—remember?—the one

14

with the Grace Kelly face and the embroidered blouse—had turned her back as Klaus Buch started to undress. Don't you remember, with sort of shoulder-length hair turned under at the ends and a braid on top that disappeared into her hair on either side of the part . . .

Helmut felt a burning envy. He had virtually never lived. There was nothing left over. Behind him there was practically nothing. If he tried to remember, he saw motionless images of streets, squares, rooms. No action. His memory-images were pervaded by a lifelessness as if in the wake of a disaster. As if the people did not yet dare to move. In any case, they stood silently against the walls. The center of the images usually remained empty. He felt that, in him, adventure had once and for all come to an end. In fact, everything worth telling. Sometimes, it was true, he would sit down and, in a kind of panic, summon a parade of all the people he had ever known. The names and faces he evoked would appear. But for the condition in which they appeared to him, the word *dead* was much too mild. Probably his memory was no worse than other people's. And, like most people, he was fascinated by his youth and childhood. But then the silent, odorless, colorless scenes would mean nothing to him. For a time he had persisted fanatically in attempting to resurrect the past. At one point he had even started to write down everything he remembered about his father, who had been a waiter at the Hindenburg Center. Helmut was disgusted when he found himself gluing together scraps of memory, coloring them, breathing onto them, inventing texts for them. He was too old for this puppet show. Surely to breathe life into the past meant resurrecting an event in a pseudo-vividness that simply denied the pastness of the past. The picture of his father that subsequently appeared on paper was a denial of the charnel-house condition in which the past existed within him. It was this very deadness of the past that interested him. Klaus Buch evidently preferred to recount the past in drastic terms. Is there anything less compatible than "past" and "drastic"? Klaus Buch was simply churning with sounds, smells, noises; the past heaved and steamed as if it were more alive than the present. Those doing the remembering became manikins pointing up to Heaven where the giants were lustily doing battle. Helmut saw only fragments, holes, wreckage, destroyed items. For many years he had done little but prepare himself to live with what had been destroyed. Nothing attracted him so much as things that had been destroyed. Someday or other he would do nothing from morning to night but surround himself with what had been destroyed. His aim was to transform his own present into a condition resembling as closely as possible the destroyed nature of the past. Already he wanted to belong to the past. That was his objective. Within him, around him, before him, he wanted everything to be as fragmentary as in the past. After all, a person is dead far longer than he is alive. It is really grotesque how tiny the present is in relation to the past. Hence this relationship should duly minimize, grind down, distort to insensibility every second of the present.

Klaus Buch and his wife ordered only steak and salad, and they ate the salad before the steak. And

they drank only mineral water. They spoke so enthusiastically about their practice of drinking mineral water that they seemed to want the Halms to follow suit at once. And what connoisseurs they were even of mineral water! Helmut had already noticed at the promenade café that they hadn't ordered coffee. They had drunk mineral water there too. But there they had not enthused about it. Out of the goodness of their hearts they rebuked Helmut and Sabina for their reckless eating and drinking habits. It was Hella who directed her reproachful concern at Sabina. Helmut and Sabina were drinking the heaviest, most expensive Pinot Noir, of which Helmut had five large glasses and Sabina two. Helmut felt himself lapsing into a delicious, somber state of languor. Far away, Klaus Buch was rehashing memories and almost fell off his chair with delight when, out of sheer politeness, Helmut went as far as to mention that the girl with the narrow braids, the theology student, whose footsteps Klaus Buch had dogged for a whole semester, had come from Worms. For this enabled Klaus to hear her voice and accent ringing in his ears again. However, in the midst of reveling in those reborn sounds, he once again let out the shriek he had uttered on the promenade; this time, since they were sitting in one of the Hecht's old, low-ceilinged rooms, the sound was so dreadful that even Helmut leaped up, that even people at other tables, even in the other rooms, leaped up. Sabina slapped Otto's nose. Klaus Buch dashed out to wash his hands. Sabina said with a sanctimonious smile: "That's the first time he's ever done that!" Although this was true, she obviously didn't believe it herself.

On his return, Klaus Buch failed to find the thread to lead him back into his orgy of memories.

For a while he and Hella looked on silently as Sabina and Helmut emptied the cheese platter, ate white bread, drank red wine. When for the third time Helmut looked up and registered the Buchs' wide-eyed horror, he said that being watched by Hella and Klaus reminded him of a scene in the life of the great Swedish philosopher Emanuel Swedenborg. Already over fifty and a famous man, he had once been having dinner alone in his room in a London hotel. Suddenly he had noticed a man in a corner of his room who at that moment called out to Swedenborg: "Don't eat so much!" And how did the great philosopher react? asked Hella. From that hour on he partook only of a roll soaked in hot milk. And a lot of coffee. But with far too much sugar. "There you are!" said Hella. "Swedenborg, Klaus—don't forget that name, he interests me. One roll per day or per meal?" "I'm sorry, I don't know," said Helmut. "That reduces the value of the diet considerably," said Hella. She seemed quite put out in her disappointment. "You've remembered everything," she said, "last name, first name, occupation, nationality, scene, location, ingredients, and then you forget the quantities. Klaus, can you understand that?" "Helmut has always been interested only in quality, never in quantity," said Klaus Buch. "But without exact quantities it's impossible to achieve quality!" cried Hella. "Don't eat so much," said Klaus Buch. Then he looked at his watch. "Good God, almost eleven!" he said. Helmut would have liked another glass or two of that wine. But Klaus Buch was already on his feet, and had paid for all of them, and, while Helmut was still protesting that he shouldn't have paid his and Sabina's share, was already announcing his plans for the next day. At six-thirty A.M. he and Hella would go for a run, at seven play tennis, then go for a sail, then have lunch, then a snooze, by three o'clock they would be rested up and ready to meet Sabina and Helmut. Of course, if Sabina and Helmut wanted to play doubles with them at seven, that would be great. Helmut declined with a shudder, Sabina with a smile.

They would have liked to give Sabina and Helmut a ride back to Nussdorf, but they had come on their bikes. Helmut felt compelled to say that he and Sabina were looking forward to the walk back. As soon as the others had left, he suggested taking the bus. But the last bus had gone. Glumly, Helmut traipsed along beside his jaunty wife toward Nussdorf. Fortunately there was a strong west wind riffling the treetops and the waters of the lake. This harmony of sound pleased him. Unfortunately Sabina was talking almost nonstop. About Klaus Buch. Although she too thought it odd that they should play tennis at seven in the morning and spurn wine and not smoke, she found the two of them refreshing. In order not to fail Sabina entirely, he said he was also quite glad they had met them, otherwise he wouldn't have had such a good wine this evening. He had never enjoyed his cigars so much as at the moment when this Klaus Buch had refused the cigar Helmut offered him, remarking that he mustn't fall from grace. "That sounded as if smoking were a crime," said Helmut, "and somehow the consciousness of committing a crime by smoking made the cigar seem to course through my veins with even greater intensity."

19

That was a lie. When he noticed their concern as they watched him smoke, his cigar had not tasted as good as usual.

For a moment Helmut wondered whether he shouldn't suggest to Sabina that they quickly undress and dash into the waves for a dip. They had done that before. But he was afraid Sabina would take the suggestion to be an effect of this Klaus Buch. She had criticized him for always saying "this Klaus Buch." What, then, would she prefer him to say? he had asked. Well, he was his friend, wasn't he? Had been, said Helmut. From age eleven to twenty-three, as he had discovered today. That meant nothing to him anymore. Even so, surely it was ridiculous to keep saying "this Klaus Buch" instead of "Klaus." "Right," said Helmut, "quite ridiculous in fact." "From now on you'll say 'Klaus,'" she said. "Yes," he said. "From now on I'll say 'Klaus.'" Sabina punched him lightly. She evidently believed they were now agreed. That was fine with him.

Because he had eaten too much and maybe also had too much to drink, his sleep was restless. Sabina also often lay awake beside him. Both were surprised that the red wine had not had a more soporific effect. Helmut said he was going into the next room to look something up. He sat down at the table and wrote: Dear Klaus Buch, I can see a misunderstanding developing. Perhaps it is already too late. That would be disastrous. I must warn you both. As soon as someone seems friendly, I have a feeling that I can no longer be as friendly as before. I believe that I now seem friendlier than I am. Sometimes I regret that I am not as friendly as I seem. If someone seems friendly, I feel as embarrassed as a meat-eater among vegetarians. I won't talk about all that has happened because that would mean soliciting empathy. I like the idea of keeping quiet about something. My ideal is to be able to look on silently when I am being misunderstood. To agree with the misunderstanding is something I would like to learn. To prefer so-called enemies to so-called friends is something I would like to learn.

Helmut stopped. He realized how absurd it was to write this letter. If he was serious about even a single sentence in this letter, he must not utter it. But he could not stop writing. So he went on: And I want you to know that I am not interested in finding out something about myself, let alone saying something about myself. That is why we should not meet again. Yes, I am running away. I know. Whoever tries to stop me will . . . I don't want to put everything into words. My heart's desire is to maintain privacy. This is a wish I share with the majority of all living people. We consort like battleships. According to less than intelligible rules. The point of these rules is their pointlessness. The more someone else knows about me, the greater would be his power over me, hence . . .

Helmut stopped. He felt relieved. The letter had acquired a tone that made it impossible for him to send it. It was only when he had pursued the tone of the letter to the point of incommunicability that he was able to stop. Now he was looking forward to bed. He felt the self-sufficiency of the negative surge through him. How wonderful that a person who has ceased to want anything is sufficient unto himself. How easy everything becomes as soon as one is alone. Not only spiritually. Every step. A glass and a hand. No problem moving. He could walk back and forth across this medallion design in the rug forever. As soon as he is alone, the tension in his shoulders is gone. Above all, the tension in his face is gone. His features relax. Lie naturally. His mouth benefits the most. It simply does what it wants. As soon as the mouth knows that we are alone, it behaves like a dog. Lies motionless for long periods, then feels like moving about, playing games. Apparently it now wants to be conscious of itself. Marvelous. Let it.

4 ⚡ By whistling, stopping to look at trees, and commenting on Birnau church lying up there so loftily and, according to him, holding out its breast to the sun like a young ox, Helmut tried to prevent their walk to the Hotel Seehalde from looking like a pilgrimage to Klaus Buch. He was trying to make something out of the walk itself. Sabina's remorseless insistence that Otto be left behind in the apartment had shocked him. That was a gesture of surrender. He had groaned, and cursed yesterday's moment of discovery by Klaus Buch. "Now come along, it'll do you good," Sabina had said. "What?" he had asked back. "To be dragged out for a change." "Dragged out of what?" "Out of your rut." "You call this a rut?" he had exclaimed, rut! This jam-packed sequence of fraught moments, every one of which in turn exacts from us a whole cluster of decisions. Shall we get up, if so, when; shall we have breakfast, but what; shall we dress, if so, how; shall we go down to the water, if so, where shall we lie down, and how. . . .

As Klaus Buch hastened toward them, Helmut put on as inscrutable an expression as possible. Klaus Buch said that, since the Halms fortunately didn't have their four-legged nuisance along, they must go sailing. Helmut looked at Sabina as if to say: Serves you right. He said it was a wonderful idea but unfortunately he and Sabina weren't dressed for sailing. Klaus said: "Off with your shoes, no problem!" Sabina simply agreed. Helmut let her see that he was surprised. Didn't she know how ridiculous they would look in a sailboat?

Helmut and Sabina were told to sit on the floorboards of the boat, which rocked violently as they stepped in. Cushions were slid beneath them. With their toes pointing skyward they sat there ill at ease, trying to dodge the expert movements of the Buchs. Klaus Buch had insisted that Sabina and Helmut also take off their stockings and socks. Otherwise they might slip and break some bones. Helmut held out his socks to Sabina while making a face in which he let despair get the upper hand. Klaus cast off, Hella tended the jib, the west wind caught the sails, Sabina was alarmed, the Buchs, who were sitting on the gunwale, laughed. Helmut felt he and Sabina were being treated like a couple of grandparents. Klaus Buch performed at the tiller as if expecting a stream of compliments. Helmut restrained himself. Gradually Sabina found that she had never imagined sailing to be so wonderful. This gentle, skimming glide, no really! And the view, Helmut, just look, from the lake the hills leaning against each other were even lovelier than when seen on a walk. She behaved as if she had never been on the lake before.

"Doesn't it look like a herd of hills camped around the lake for a rest?" she cried. Evidently she was trying to compete with Klaus in picturesque speech. Helmut also responded to the gentleness of the hills they were sailing past but took care not to say so. Klaus Buch said it. He knew his Helmut, he said. No one could tell him that he, Helmut, would remain untouched by the green contours rising and falling in the dazzling sunlight. At school, Helmut had always written the most soulful mood-prose. But his cleverest trick had been to read aloud the most outlandish phrases in a totally dispassionate voice.

It pleased Helmut to be enthused over so inaccurately. For Sabina's sake as well. He noticed that his feet were ice-cold. It was a hot day. Discreetly he tried to move his feet into the sun.

All he could think of was to ask Klaus Buch about his career. He hoped that, in talking about himself, Klaus Buch would moderate his language. Indeed, when he talked about himself, it was less flamboyant than when he had talked about Helmut. But the way he characterized himself also grated on Helmut. Whatever that fellow did was wrong. Blithely Klaus Buch confessed that he had not found himself equipped by nature to be an educator. Had he become a teacher, he wouldn't have had the willpower required to keep out of a rut. A run-of-the-mill bourgeois, that's what he would have become. A narrow-minded, disintegrating concentrate of uric acid, that's all. Without challenge he couldn't exist. If he was not overtaxed, he wasn't alive. He needed to be stretched to his limits to be aware of himself. So he had become a journalist. A specialist in environmental problems. And in ecology, a specialist in nutrition. On television too. Sabina said at once that they hardly ever watched TV because they spent their evenings reading. Klaus envied Sabina and Helmut. To read in the evenings, beautiful. It comforted him to think that such people still existed. Hella said: "In your *All Things Green* you say: 'Readers are mankind's green lung.'" "Hella," he said, "fancy you knowing me by heart! I believe you do still care for me a little." That was his favorite among all his books, his *All Things Green*. But what do the Halms read, in the evening? "De Sade," said Helmut quickly, before Sabina could reply. "And Masoch," Sabina chimed in sulkily. "What a pair you are!" exclaimed Klaus. Helmut said: "That's right." "Ready about!" cried Klaus. "Ready!" cried Hella. "Hard alee!" cried Klaus. Sabina and Helmut ducked.

"You know, Klaus," said Sabina (Helmut was annoyed because she always addressed Klaus Buch as Klaus; he had persisted in calling Hella Mrs. Buch and, on being ordered by her husband to call her Hella, had avoided her first name altogether), "for years Helmut has been intending to write two books, but the school simply ties him down; now he has reduced his plans to one book, but even that, he has to keep postponing." "You know what, Hella," said Klaus, "we'll present the Halms with our inoffensive little books." "Yes, do!" cried Sabina. "Helmut, maybe that will encourage you to make a start."

Helmut was thinking that, although it might be a kind of vice, surely it was the sweetest of all feelings to find that even your own wife was totally in the dark about you. Naturally he nodded to everything that Klaus said, that Sabina said and, as a sign of intellectual respect, raised his eyebrows to the very top of his forehead. So Helene Buch has also written a book. You don't say! On herbs. And Klaus has published quite a number. On food in general. Well, well. And there are seventy-five thousand people eating according to his theories. That's the way it is. But he has remained modest. He claimed no merit for it. He had just put into words what was in the air anyway. Hella's book on herbs had far greater merit and thus a much smaller readership. Hella protested. "I would never have written a book if he hadn't insisted. Besides, I didn't really write a book, I merely translated Pastor Künzle into modern German—I mean, whenever he mentions God I've replaced it with Nature. I expect you know *Herbes and Weedes*? No?!" Well, that was why the Buchs had been coming to this area for three years, to gain more insight into Pastor Künzle's ideas. Spiritually, too, as it were. Pastor Künzle had suddenly become more important to them than Byzantium or Ravenna. Meanwhile Klaus had become so enamored of the area that he was planning a big book about Lake Constance, to be called: *Let Europe Drink Thy Waters*.

Klaus Buch said it was time to put an end to that fraud over there. He pointed to the prehistoric lake dwellings of Unteruhldingen that they happened to be passing. "What do you mean, fraud?" asked Helmut. He thought he remembered reading in the brochure that these pile dwellings in the lake were, quite frankly, built in 1929 or 1930. "The fraud," said Klaus, "is that there never were any lake dwellings there," whereas these phony lake dwellings were meant to give the impression that at one time there had been. Did he know for sure, Helmut asked, that there had never been any lake dwellings

27

at this or some other nearby spot, perhaps off Gold-
bach or Süssenmühle? At no time and at no place
along or in Lake Constance had there ever been any
prehistoric lake dwellings. Helmut said with a
smile: "My dear Klaus Buch, there were no lake
dwellings here during the Stone Age?" Generally
speaking, the indigenous Celtic population had not
gone in for pile dwellings; wouldn't the barbarous
Alemanni hordes have immediately swept them
away? Helmut had no idea. But Klaus Buch's tone
goaded him to contradict. "Yes yes ye-es!" cried
Klaus Buch. "That's exactly what that swindler
would like to hear! The man who invented it all, and
as a result was made a professor forty years ago,
could hug himself because his clumsy and hence
successful inventions must have long since made
him a millionaire. Mind you, it's pure envy on my
part, I admit that. If I felt the urge to achieve something, it would be a fraud with a solid foundation,
a real live proposition." "But haven't you achieved
that?" laughed Hella. "The seventy-five thousand
people who eat according to your books are pretty
real, aren't they?" For a moment he looked at Hella
aghast—his tongue was working against the inside
of his upper lip, bulging it out as if the tongue were
imprisoned there—then he laughed, louder than
Hella had laughed. Then he said that was what you
got for marrying a callow young thing like that. His
first wife could never have been so devoid of in-
stinct as to take seriously an ironical remark which
he had made about himself and then turn it against
him. Herta had made a lot of mistakes, but not that
one. Never. But unfortunately she had never developed and for that reason had begrudged him his

own development, that was why he had had to leave her if he didn't want to wither like a plant in a pot that was too small for it. Klaus Buch directed these explanations at Sabina. Then he turned to Hella, and said in a deadly serious, utterly hopeless, tone: "You don't care for me anymore, do you?" She laughed at him, leaned across and kissed him. He quickly turned his head so that her kiss landed on his mouth. Then he ran his tongue all around his lips so as not to lose one particle of Hella's kiss. Helmut found it hard not to look only at Hella. He had to look carefully past her because the others might have noticed how insatiable his eyes were. But then, of course, he was an expert at looking past people.

His feet still felt cold although they were now lying in the sun. That was to say, only part of his feet. Only the heels. But they were as cold as if lying in snow. He should have moved about. He and Sabina were sitting there like a corner-grocery couple who had been talked into taking much too arduous a boat trip to celebrate their golden anniversary. They must look a scream, sitting on little cushions on the floorboards, their bare feet stretched out in front of them. The misshapen toes. The horribly reddened skin.

At first, the separation from his children had been a real body blow, said Klaus Buch, raising his face into the wind and screwing up his eyes so that the golden eyelashes met intrepidly. His wife, a fanatical bourgeois, had set the kids against him to such an extent that they refused to have anything more to do with him. Hella, he was glad to say, thought the way he did: no kids on any account. To screw only to produce children: how square can you get—right? He was sure that Helmut, who, even as a boy, had been past master of the bizarre, had developed a gorgeously lurid, heavily ritualized art of screwing. It was a good thing that nowadays everyone could screw to his own taste. Hella and he, for instance, were into bouncing. That had literally nauseated his first wife. Man was no doubt a mistake on the part of Nature, but bourgeois man was the elevation of this mistake to a program. Uptight like Hitler, stupid like a Bavarian prime minister, and wicked like Stalin. Hella and he could hardly wait for the day when they could finally turn their backs on this bourgeois country. The income from one more apartment building and they would put out to sea. Set their course for the Bahamas. There was simply no hope for the Germans. Take his first wife, for example: an admirer of Pius XII. At fourteen, a Holy Year pilgrim, with her father, an audience with the Pope. She never recovered from that. Favorite book: *Richard Wagner's Letters to Mathilde Wesendonck.* Next most favorite: *The Song of Bernadette* by Werfel. And knew on Monday morning which blouse she would wear on Friday. Hella looked at her Klaus with compassion. Sabina said as ironically as she could: "How enviable!" Klaus Buch shouted: "Ready about!" Hella shouted "Ready!" Klaus Buch shouted: "Hard alee!" Sabina and Helmut ducked.

Suddenly Hella removed her top, tucked it away saying that with this wind Klaus could manage alone, and lay down on the bow. Resorting to his professional glance, Helmut observed her breasts as he looked past them. The breasts looked as if they were inquisitive too. Fortunately Klaus Buch had gone on talking as if nothing had happened. Did the Halms have any children? Helmut said: "Sabina, do we have any children?" Sabina said that if he were to ask their two children whether they had any parents, they would probably answer: "Parents! For God's sake, never had any!" When he had seen their dog, said Klaus Buch, he had taken them for a childless couple. "Why don't you two have a dog?" Sabina asked. They avoided anything which might interfere with their independence, said Klaus Buch. If one morning they should feel like flying to Tenerife, they must be in a position to leave their little house in Starnberg at noon and land in Los Rodeos that evening, otherwise he would simply feel like a cockroach. And that wasn't a pleasant feeling. At school he had often felt like a cockroach. In those days, Helmut had been pretty good at making him squirm. Just because his parents had had a big house on the hill, with a garden full of plum trees and a blackberry patch, Helmut had refused ever to set foot on the Buch property, and had even tried, sometimes successfully, to incite the other kids not to walk home with Klaus Buch. He had been all for the class struggle, said Klaus Buch. "Not anymore," said Sabina dryly. "Too bad," said Klaus Buch. At that time, of course, he hadn't been able to understand Helmut's secret hatred for the Buch property. He had thought it was directed at him personally. If during their group masturbation he hadn't been able to prove that his penis was the equal of any other, he would really have been desperate. My God, what would he have done if it hadn't been for that masturbating in the school toilet and on the construction sites. Those had been just about his only chances for rehabilitation. Since he had been shorter than most of the other kids, they had naturally assumed that everything they had was longer than what he had. But he'd shown them up nicely. Did Helmut remember, when the new bank was being built, on the top floor? Objective: who can manage to pee through the skylight opening? And who was the first to do it? Little Klaus Buch. Yes indeed. What those bean poles lacked was either pressure or firmness to produce the necessary range. No amount of math could produce that parabola. But the one who got the biggest laugh had been Helmut, Klaus Buch cried ecstatically. Helmut shuddered at his tone. For in those days Helmut had had—something he surely no longer was bothered with—a knotty problem with his foreskin. A real little cauliflower of a foreskin at the orifice, that's what Helmut had had. Needless to say, that had interfered with a fine, long-range jet. Only a sort of intermittent gush. Pulling it back was unfeasible. Much too painful. So what does our Helmut do? Takes his thumb and forefinger and pinches the skin in front firmly together. Lets his water come. Holds on tight. The skin-balloon fills and fills. And when it's about to burst, our HH fires away. But unfortunately in the wrong direction. Sheer ambition has made our HH aim steeper than steep and he squirts the whole lot into his own face. Klaus Buch laughed and laughed and repeated the more dramatic bits. Sabina had merely let out a shriek. Helene Buch laughed her high-pitched, penetrating laugh. Helmut commanded himself to laugh loudest and longest. He succeeded.

"One of the finest moments of our erotic dawn," said Klaus Buch in an even more brimming voice, "occurred in the cellar of—remember?— Rolf Eberle, d'you remember, on Rothenwald Street when we tried again. The rest were all rubbing away nicely, it was dark of course, we couldn't turn on the light, or talk, so we thought we all had the delicious agony of our lust well under way when suddenly we heard Helmut's voice saying very, very softly: "Now I've got to the real thing."

Again he burst out laughing. Hella said: "How adorable!" Sabina said: "You were a fine bunch, I must say!" Helmut laughed an operatic, full-throated Ha-ha-ha-haaa! Klaus repeated the words Helmut was supposed to have said and explained that everyone in that cellar had immediately grasped that for the first time our HH had managed to pull back his foreskin over the glans. *Ecco!*

Sabina said she was simply amazed that Klaus should remember everything in such detail. "Aren't you, Helmut?"

"Congratulations, Klaus," said Helmut. "As you see, you've already convinced Sabina that what you've been describing actually happened."

"Didn't it?" asked Klaus.

"Not that I know of," said Helmut, and was annoyed at the level tone of his voice.

"Oh how disappointing, Helmut," said Klaus Buch, "to find you trying to deny these touching childhood moments."

"I tell you, I simply don't remember a thing about them," Helmut said. "I couldn't tell you it was like that or it wasn't like that. So you can say whatever you like, I can only listen and marvel. I'm sure you didn't have an easy time with us in those days. You were a bit isolated, I seem to remember. Ever since you had the bike with the balloon tires, I think. That may have stimulated your imagination. An entirely normal process, actually. Everyone tends to compensate."

Sabina yawned pointedly.

"Helmut, that's a point I'm going to have to tackle you on," Klaus Buch said. "It doesn't have to be now. But trying to turn the most sacred moments of our childhood into figments of my imagination—I'm not going to let you get away with that. Those childhood flickerings can't simply be stamped out."

Hella said as if from a higher plane: "Sailing over the water and reviving old memories, how absolutely out of this world! I never knew how well they went together. Water and memories. Now really, Helmut," she said, punching his shoulder, "the reason these dear little vignettes have surfaced in Klaus's mind today is because *you* are here. I never knew about the five-finger exercises of those little men. By himself, he wouldn't have either. Otherwise he would have told me. He tells me everything, you know. Everything he has been telling us was prompted by you. And now you want to take it away from him again. Don't tell me you're a sadist too?" Meets Klaus's eyes. Then: "Forgive me, darling, I didn't mean to say that. It just slipped out." Helmut said: "Never mind, I'll let him have his puppet show." Hella rewarded him with a kiss on his temple. Sabina said: "Don't spoil him." "How glorious it all is!" exclaimed Klaus Buch. "God, who would ever have thought life could be so beautiful! And the most beautiful part, to my mind, is that it could have been different too. Something had to be done to make it as beautiful as it is at this moment. At this very moment, dear friends, we have reached the peak! And if from now on anyone in this boat uses anything but first names, overboard he goes. According to the law of the sea, the captain's orders must be implicitly obeyed. Ready about! Ready! Hard alee!"

With the change in course, Helmut's feet were in the shade again. He stretched them out into the sun. His heels remained ice-cold.

When they had docked, Sabina said that the effects of going sailing surpassed her wildest dreams. Seen from the shore, sailing often looked as if nothing at all were happening out there. Now she felt drunk. But in the most agreeable way. She felt so light and yet so heavy. And how aware she was of her skin! Never before had she been so aware of her skin. She felt as if she had been on Mount Olympus for a massage and was now returning to earth, growing heavier by the minute. "Regards from Apollo the masseur," said Helmut. But he agreed with his wife that the effects of such a sail were unimaginable for a nonsailor. He, too, felt as if he had been thoroughly worked over. Only he couldn't yet say by whom or what. It surely hadn't been Apollo. But it might well have been a god. At any rate he would like to thank Hella and Klaus Buch most warmly for having put up with him and Sabina so patiently in their boat, and he hoped they would both thoroughly enjoy the rest of their vacation. Klaus Buch would not accept that.

Parting company? What? What's that? Oh I see, one of those typical HH-notions. Is that how it was meant? "He's a sadist, we know that," said Hella.

"Sometimes he tries to overdo it," said Sabina.

"I see we're agreed," said Klaus. "Man, was that ever a shock! 'We hope you will both thoroughly enjoy . . .' I've a good mind to beat you up." Half in fun, half in earnest, he started pummeling Helmut.

"Very well then," he said, "since Helmut quite rightly feels that whenever I watch him eating I want to keep saying 'Don't eat so much,' we'll meet after supper. . . ."

"Hey, wait a moment, what was the name of that fellow with the rolls?" cried Helene. "Sweden-borg," said Sabina. "This time I'll write it down myself," said Hella. "That Klaus has a memory like a hole." "Like a sieve, if you don't mind, I don't let the big pieces through," said Klaus. "No sweat, then you'll remember Swedenborg," said Helmut. "Okay, eight-thirty then," said Hella. Helmut drew Sabina away.

"We'll be there to pick you up!" Klaus Buch called. It sounded like a threat.

"Ye-es!" Sabina called back. It sounded like an endearment.

Helmut and Sabina tramped off to their apartment. As soon as they get away from those Buchs, life becomes humdrum, dreary, the fire goes out. Nonsense. You should say the very opposite. Helmut swore. That wretch Sabina: why hadn't she helped him to ward off the attacks of that dieting, sailing athlete? Sabina feigned surprise. Hadn't

Helmut, just a few moments ago, lavished praise on the afternoon? Surely he wouldn't have done that if he had disliked the Buchs, or would he? "I would," he said. "Yes," she said, "you're quite capable of that."

5 ◄ *Helmut bullied* Sabina into being
ready in good time. By eight twenty-five they were
standing outside the low garden gate. Beside the
garbage cans. So it must be Monday evening. In all
those eleven years he had never once managed to
carry out the garbage cans. Whenever he went to do
so, Mrs. Zürn had already carried them out. He
would have liked at least once to carry out the
Zürns' garbage cans with their own. To seem help-
ful would have amused him.

"You're always in such a rush," said Sabina.
"Now we're standing here like two bumps on a
log." He couldn't tell her that under no circumstances would he allow Klaus Buch and Helene to
set foot in their apartment here at the Zürns'. If they
were ever to set foot in that apartment he would
never again spend his vacation here. Why, he didn't
know. That was why he couldn't discuss it with
Sabina. To apologize for his seemingly senseless
haste, he quickly ran his thumb along the hollow of
her neck. Her head drooped toward her responsive
shoulders, her eyebrows rose, her body relaxed
into an **S**.

The Buchs drove up, jumped out, greeted them
as if they hadn't seen each other for years. Back in
the apartment, Otto barked and howled. "Poor
thing," said Helene.

"You're right," said Helmut.

"Klaus, if you would watch your hands a little more carefully, we could take him along," said Helene.

"Thanks a lot, and I can always wear gloves, of course," said Klaus.

"Because of you the poor dog has to spend all evening—"

"Okay, okay," he interrupted, "by all means bring him out!"

"No!" Sabina cried.

"Well said!" exclaimed Helmut, and ran into the house to fetch Otto, who was jumping for joy.

"Otto!" cried Sabina. "Down, Otto, down!"

Helmut congratulated Klaus on his self-control.

Before very long, Helmut managed to steer the stroll along the promenade into a wine tavern. He confessed that he had never had anything else in mind: the idea of having to spend an evening without wine simply paralyzed him.

"So we're not enough for you," said Helene.

Helmut hesitated, looked at Hella a shade too long, and said with a quiet shake of his head: "No."

"*Prosit,*" said Sabina in a conciliatory tone.

The Halms drank wine, the Buchs drank water. Helmut couldn't understand how, in the ensuing discussion about wine and water, the Buchs could become so animated. He always drank his first glass rather quickly because, until he had had a drink, he didn't feel the slightest desire to open his mouth.

Suddenly Klaus Buch yelled: "No!" Sabina said: "Now it's happened." Helmut shouted: "Otto, down." Klaus Buch stood holding up one hand with the other as if it were seriously injured.

Hella said: "Oh for God's sake, Klaus!"

Klaus, still clutching his hand, said: "He's got

such a cold, wet tongue, Christ you've no idea. And always me, why always me? Can you explain that?"

Helmut said: "No."

Sabina said: "This is the last time we take him along. That's it." And down to Otto: "Bad dog."

Hella said: "Poor Otto. I really feel sorry for him."

"For whom?" Klaus Buch cried.

Hella said: "For you too, of course, darling."

Helmut said brightly: "There is nothing one can't feel sorry for."

Klaus Buch said: "All right, now I'm putting my hands on the table; if anyone sees me taking a hand off the table by mistake, please tell me immediately."

It struck Helmut that, in relation to his almost fragile build, Klaus Buch had noticeably heavy wrists. And his forearms: manifestly more powerful than his own. And the hands, broader. The fingers, stronger. No question that he also had a larger, more efficient penis. Nevertheless it was Helmut's impression that Hella would have enjoyed poking fun at her husband's obsession with his physical fitness.

And invariably when she looked across at him with a less than lovesick expression, he would immediately say in a despondent voice: "You don't care for me anymore, do you." And she would invariably pucker up her lips and blow him a kiss. Helmut had the feeling that in blowing the kiss she didn't care where it landed. But it was enough to see their tanned arms and hands, and Helmut's and Sabina's arms and hands, lying on the table to know who belonged to whom.

Helmut noticed that today his cigars and wine

were less enjoyable than the day before. He was afraid he would not be able to defend his habits against this couple. They attacked him ceaselessly. Both of them. They were getting him down. It was enough to sit at the same table with them to feel in the wrong. Meanwhile Hella was cradling Klaus Buch's hands in her own; in fact, she was cradling all of him. He was somehow snuggled up under her arm, his head against her breast. Helmut and Sabina noted simultaneously that Klaus was falling asleep.

"Ssh," said Sabina. "He's asleep."

Hella explained that every morning for the past few days Klaus had run five times around the track at the marina, she being the timekeeper; his best time was 5:11, which meant Klaus must have considered himself a superchampion runner; 2,000 meters in 5:11, that equaled, say, the best Russian time of that year. But this morning Klaus had been told by some horrible old gymnast that the track was not 400 meters long, as one had a right to expect, but only 300, so that Klaus hadn't run 2,000 meters but only 1,500. She could have killed that cynical old gymnast. Couldn't he have kept his stupid remark to himself? Klaus murmured: "Helmut, please, do tell me, what was it our physics teacher used to call out on the first floor?" Helmut didn't know. "Come on, Helmut," groaned Klaus, displaying an agonized face, "our physics teacher who always shouted: 'The lower floor belongs to me!' Something like that. 'The first floor is my domain!' Some such thing. I need the actual words. If you don't get every single word right, you have nothing. One word in the wrong place, and the whole sentence is hollow, dead. As soon as you get the word in the right place, *Open Sesame!* There stands our teacher, shouting his head off, there *you* stand, clear as day. Won't you help me, Helmut?—please!"

"For God's sake help him, can't you see how he's suffering?" said Hella. "He's turning all blue with lack of memory-oxygen. Helmut!"

Helmut said automatically: "The whole lower floor belongs to physics." "Right, Helmut, right!" shouted Klaus Buch, whereupon he leaped up, fell on Helmut's neck, and continued to whimper "Right." And blissfully repeated: "The whole lower floor belongs to physics." Helmut looked at Hella over Klaus Buch's shoulder, trying to convey that she alone had dredged up the words of a long-dead physics instructor from the depths of thirty years. Klaus murmured happily: "Call the waitress." Helmut shouted in positive alarm: "The check, please. All on one!"

Klaus held his hand horizontally across both eyes. He was playing the role of someone who refuses to witness a disaster. Hella, as she stroked her Klaus with exaggerated motherly concern, said that now the Halms had really and truly offended her Klaus. Without the slightest warning she had lapsed into a grotesque Swabian accent. Klaus straightened up and covered his ears. Hella intensified her grotesque accent as she informed them that it was really torture for Klaus when she imitated his native dialect. Klaus Buch sprang to his feet, whereupon Hella, in an equally grotesque Bavarian accent, said that Klaus was a loony mutt and shouldn't carry on like that, if she had a piano now she would leave him in peace. With her Bavarian accent her face acquired, as if demanded by the dialect, an angry expression. Klaus was now standing in front of her as if to hypnotize her. She said: "Don't you look at me like that, my boy!" and ran her fingers across his eyes. Klaus said: "You don't care for me anymore, do you." She kissed him. They could leave now.

The Buchs tried to talk Helmut and Sabina into a game of tennis. That was successfully warded off. All right, then they would all go on a hike together. The Buchs would be at the Halms' place at eight— "Nine!" Helmut cried shrilly. With their car. Since the Halms had been coming to this area for eleven years, they must know of some good hikes, so it was Helmut's job to come up with some inspiration overnight.

As Helmut lay behind the wonderfully straight bars on the windows of their ground-floor apartment, he felt happy again. Fortunately Sabina had immediately reached for her Wagner—*My Life*. Fortunately she had made no attempt to touch him. He hoped she was lying beside him as he beside her. That would be life's crowning achievement. For each of them. If he could have been sure that Sabina had reached the same point as he had, he would now have said how pleasant it was to be lying in this isolated apartment. He would have liked to give vent to the thought of how terrible it would be to be lying under the same roof as the Buchs. But then Sabina would have asked, Why? And then it might have turned out that Sabina had not yet reached the same point as he had.

Helmut recalled a night twelve years ago, during the last vacation they had spent in Italy. In a hotel in Grado. They were just about to come together when from the next room he heard a noise as of a bed being struck by a giant hammer. Every blow went clearly through all the springs and ended up hard. The amazing thing about this noise, in view of the presumed force of the hammer blows, was the speed, the incredible speed, with which the blows fell. Helmut had guessed at once that he would never find his own rhythm as long as that fellow next door kept hammering away like that. He had noticed that Sabina was also listening intently. Surely she must, must, *must* reproach him for not being that kind of a hammer. They both lay there, just listening to what a man is capable of. Helmut wouldn't have believed it possible. Should he count the blows? He was suffocating with heat. He was dreadfully embarrassed. He was at fault. The fellow next door was in tune with the times. That's how a man must have felt in the old days of the pillory. Anyone falling short of the sexual demands of this age and of society was, so to speak, permanently pilloried. There were enough publications to take care of that. With words and pictures. Now to escape. Where to? To kill. Her. Strangle her. But his hands didn't move. The hammering seemed to be going on indefinitely. It simply never stopped. He gasped for air. He found he had been holding his breath. Later he told himself that the whole thing could have lasted no more than eleven or twenty-one or at most twenty-nine minutes. But as long as it lasted it seemed as if it would never, never stop. If at least he could have thought of some words to release Sabina and himself from the spell of sheer listening. He could think of nothing. Spellbound, they had been forced to listen until it was over. If they were now sleeping in the same hotel as Klaus and Helene Buch, Sabina would be sure to imagine what the Buchs were doing, and involuntarily Klaus Buch and that episode in the Italian hotel would merge, blend, and Klaus Buch would then be that other fellow. The Buchs were into bouncing. Whatever that is, thought Helmut, it doesn't concern me. But Sabina. Sabina was the point at which he was vulnerable. Did he want to be able to compete? When he read about the level of performance required in order not to be considered impotent, he felt pilloried. For months he had not felt inclined to give way to his sexuality. The mere fact of those people publicly prescribing to each other how often they had to crawl onto their wives in order not to be considered impotent was enough to arouse his aversion and disgust. Whenever he felt the urge to have sex, he had only to think of that terrible propaganda to calm down again. He hoped all this would soon be behind him. But until he had discussed it with Sabina, nothing was behind him. He should have told her long ago what it was that interfered when he wanted to come to her. The moment he thought of her, wanted to touch her, something in his mind prevented him. Then it seemed utterly ridiculous to roll across to her, or to send his hand on ahead, or to ask Sabina outright, or to start a seductive conversation. Nothing would then seem as unbearably comical as any activity determined by or directed toward sexuality. And he had a feeling that this had something to do with the way in which these activities were publicly recommended. To desire it, yes. To do it, no. That the day would come when he would no longer desire it was more than he dared hope. It would probably always remain a kind of open wound. He would at least have to tell Sabina he couldn't lie quietly beside her unless he was sure she was lying quietly beside him. He wanted to give her a sign. So he carefully moved his hand toward her and let it lie close to her shoulder. He didn't envy Klaus Buch what he was no doubt at this very instant actively engaged in. Or did he? He had no definite opinion about these profoundly stirring sensations, much less a categorical, or categorically negative, one. As a teacher he was an eloquent supporter of society's insistence on greater sexual freedom. Wasn't he considered progressive? This was an area where he could hang onto his incognito. He was considered very progressive. He invoked the right to freedom of opinion as his justification. Surely in his domestic and most private life he didn't have to put into practice the pretense he maintained in school. Wasn't society's insistence on greater sexual freedom conceived to make each person responsible for the measure of his own lust? Just as marks you get in school are your own responsibility. As a teacher he felt justified in condemning sexual indifference, which is how society wanted it, whereas at home he felt justified in trying to condemn sexual pleasure, which is how he wanted it. No criticism implied of the national or popular dailies, parliament, and school. How were people supposed to get through life without pretense? Didn't he know how difficult it was to escape the dominance of pretense even for an instant, or even to a minute degree or even tentatively? Immediately you feel pilloried. So, quick march back to the pleasure front, the leisure front, the pretense-production front. But again and again this temptation to escape. Apart from Sabina, no one must notice it. She even had to help him, otherwise he wouldn't get away. In school he would continue to produce the required pretenses. But at home he would let himself go. He had already given a name to the state which he would then attain: martyred inertia. It was his favorite mood. There he perceived his entire heaviness, but with approval. That heaviness, sweating a bit. With approval. Heavy and sweating and pale. The color, too, he perceived with approval. Color of a corpse. With approval. Himself a heavy, sweating corpse, that was his favorite mood, martyred inertia. How to involve Sabina? She was probably still living under the full force of the dictate of pretense. She must be given an inkling of the opposite. Self-indulgence, she would say. Sabina with her social commitment; that's to say, the commitment serving the production of social pretense. He noted that revulsion was channeling his thoughts. He had nothing to worry about: he had his revulsion. His position behind the position. He had his pleasure in being misunderstood. Deception, wasn't that the essence of all that was required? The goal of producing pretense! With his well-developed talent for deception and the pleasure he took in deception, wasn't he a paragon of all that was desired here and now? So much for solitude, self-indulgence, remoteness! Representative, that's what he was! Quintessentially typical, that's what he was! He was the prototype! Fine. Had he attained it, was he enjoying it now, his martyred inertia? Almost, yes, almost.

Unfortunately, this glorious mood was very susceptible to temperature. It had to be warm. He had to feel warm. The slightest hint of cold was enough to destroy everything. The fact that his feet were still cold bothered him. One must be aware of no unpleasant sensation, then one was *there*. He couldn't understand why his feet simply wouldn't get warm. They were painfully cold. He put on his

socks. Sabina, who was still reading her Wagner—
My Life, asked what was the matter. "Cold feet," he
said bluntly. But the socks made his feet colder
rather than warmer. "Goddam synthetics," he said,
ripping his socks off, and went to get his wool
sweater, in which he wrapped his feet. When he
touched one foot with the other, he noticed that
both feet were warm. Even so, in each separate foot
he felt a chill that was positively painful.

Sabina put aside her book and stretched out a
hand. He gave it a quick squeeze and tried to give
it back to her. But she immediately stretched out
her hand again. "No, let me," she said, in a tone to
which, in his opinion, she was no longer entitled. So
he let her hand lie on his shoulder. He had with-
drawn his own hand. He would turn away imperceptibly so as to get rid of her hand, which now
bothered him. But Sabina noticed his intention. Apparently she was concentrating fully on the hand
lying on Helmut's shoulder. This hand was her float
that signaled whether she had a bite. He wouldn't
bite. What was she thinking of anyway, suddenly
trying to start something again at this point? Surely
he could assume that the tentative state he had so
happily achieved had been reached not entirely
without her consent. If she continued to maneuver
her hand like that, he would have to ask her to
account for her backsliding. He really had no alter-
native. She wouldn't stop. And if he said nothing,
she would assume she was making progress. And if
she allowed her expectations to grow, he would
have to pay for it. Maybe this was the time for that
overdue talk. "What's got into you, Sabina?" he
said quietly. She responded with sounds he would
rather not have heard. Outside in the darkness

there was thunder and lightning. A thunderstorm. That's all we need. She probably considered a thunderstorm an encouraging sign. Or even—if she was that far gone already—an open invitation. But then Sabina wasn't a Wagnerian. "Okay, then I'll ask Klaus if he'll sleep with me," she said. For God's sake, woman, he thought, don't say that. Very slowly and as gently as possible he went: "Sssssssh." Then he stroked her head. Just her hair. Unmistakably soothing. Distracting. Suddenly the rain came splashing down. He considered that a deliverance. Slowly, slowly he withdrew his hand. He pulled up his knees, sought his knees with his chin, made himself as small as possible. He had the feeling that for the last few years he had been living alone. Sabina, he thought, can you hear me? He had hurt her, a moment ago. He was incapable of movement. He lay rigid. With fear. They were so close to one another that every hurt he inflicted on her felt as if it were being inflicted on himself. It was only much later, when he could be sure that Sabina had fallen asleep, that his body relaxed. He could think about falling asleep himself.

He dreamed he was turning over in his coffin and that, in spite of the complete darkness, he sensed that one side of the coffin was missing. This impression was so vivid that one of his hands began to grope toward the side that seemed to be missing. Sure enough, it wasn't there. Immediately, an upward movement followed, faster now. The coffin lid was there. But where the side was missing his hand kept groping apprehensively. It touched a step. He had to push himself up and came to lie on the step outside the coffin. He mustn't stay there. Involuntarily he rolled down on the other side of the step

49

and lay where he landed. But now he realized that he was in a hall from which it was possible to get out. This suited him. He knew he would emerge into daylight, among people. And he knew there was only one condition: if even a single person recognizes you, it's all over, forever. He woke up in terror and thought: the new life.

6 ⚡ *At five minutes* to nine, Helmut and Sabina were standing on the porch, watching fat bumblebees crawl into the delicate blossoms. Helmut joked about the bumblebees' little polleny pants. He was trying to bring a smile to Sabina's face before the Buchs arrived. He didn't succeed. Not until the beautiful old silver Mercedes 230 coupé pulled over did she smile. The women had to find room in the narrow back seat. Helmut said it did him good to see the women squeezed in like that. "Must've read too much de Sade last night," said Klaus Buch. "That's why you haven't left your four-legged torturer behind, too." If that creature was going to snap at Klaus's hand when it happened to be changing gears, a disaster was inevitable. "At last a disaster," said Helmut. "We'll leave him behind," said Sabina. "Stop griping and get going," said Hella.

"You don't care for me anymore, do you," said Klaus in his despondent voice. "Where are we going anyway?" "Up onto the Höchste," said Helmut, and gave him directions.

But Klaus wouldn't reach for the gear shift for fear that Otto would take the opportunity to lick his hand. "We'll leave him behind!" Sabina almost screamed. Hella, her voice even shriller: "I'll drive!" Klaus Buch had to sit in the back. Now Hella found she hadn't brought along her glasses. Sabina offered hers. Hella tried them on. To everyone's joy, they were suitable. "How beautifully they distort you," said Klaus. Hella stroked Otto. Helmut liked that. "The countryside inland," he said, "is a paradise."

He promised them a hike through magnificent, silent forests. Then a view ranging from the Vorarlberg to Bern. He could feel his voice verging on the rhapsodic. Walking in the forest would be like walking in a cathedral. Only that the light would be more vivid and the air better. The most important thing about these forests was that they could still evoke that old feeling of infinity.

In Limpach he told Hella to stop and jumped out of the car. Suddenly he was seized by an eagerness that surprised even him. He couldn't remember whether this was the spot where he and Sabina had started out on their hike, but he tried to pretend that he was quite sure and made them all get out. That's right, they would start walking from here. Into the forest. In the forest he turned off the paved road. After five minutes the undergrowth became impenetrable. Otto ran off out of the forest. They followed him. Meanwhile it had started to rain. Since progress between forest edge and meadow was also laborious, they ran—Helmut again took the lead—across the meadow toward a clump of trees where there was a crucifix. Helmut hoped to be able to wait out the rain here and then continue their walk along a field path. Beneath the trees there was a bench onto which they subsided with relief. Helmut had no idea where they were. Klaus Buch reminded them that, on leaving the car, he had asked what they would do if it rained. We would be walking through the magnificent, cathedral-like, luminous, aromatic infinity-forest, Helmut had intoned. And now, where was that forest, so magnificent, tall, luminous, aromatic, and filled with infinity? Farther up they would come to a forest like that, said Helmut, shouting rather than speaking. He was, quite simply, aroused. How much farther up? Three hundred yards maybe, did they have to argue about every foot of the way, with the rain about to stop anyway? Was it now, said Klaus Buch, and where did he think the weather was coming from? They all looked at him. From the west, Helmut said in a voice conveying patient indulgence toward the questioner.

"Not so!" cried Klaus Buch, in a voice that implied: Ha! "Helmut says it'll stop any minute," said Klaus Buch, "because he's only looking toward the west, where the sky is clear. But the least he could do is lick his finger and hold it up into the wind, then he'd know that today the weather's coming from the east. Now listen to me: we'll start running right now, in ten minutes it'll be raining so hard that we'll have no protection here." "But where do we run to?" asked the women. And it was Klaus Buch they asked. Over there, he said, behind some trees he had glimpsed a farm roof. And he was already running ahead. The women followed. Otto scampered after Sabina. So Helmut had no choice but to follow.

Wet with rain and sweat, they paused for breath under the overhanging barn roof. Klaus Buch, having arrived long before the women and Helmut, greeted them with a laugh. He didn't seem in the least out of breath. Well, there were worse things than a forest in this rain, he shouted, for it would soon be raining harder than ever. Over there, that wall of cloud, there was more to come. The only thing to do was to strip to the waist and run up the hill, so they would have something dry to put on when they got to the top. As he spoke, he was already undressing. So was Hella. Helmut hoped no one would come out of the farmhouse. Since Hella wasn't wearing a bra, she was naked to the waist after taking off her jacket and blouse. Here her breasts seemed even more inquisitive than on the boat. Again Helmut looked at them by looking past them. He and Sabina maintained that they always walked fully dressed in the rain. They were so used to it. Was there anything nicer than a warm summer rain?

Klaus started running. They reached the paved road and headed as fast as they could for the hilltop restaurant. By the time Helmut and Sabina arrived with Otto, Klaus Buch was already standing at the door, fresh as a daisy, his hair combed. Helmut was soaked with sweat as much as with rain. He was panting. Sabina was also a pitiful sight. Klaus Buch laughed and said it was a good thing Helmut had been the one to plan the hike. Helmut said as breezily as possible: "Oh, it was me, that's right." "It was your idea to come up here," said Klaus Buch, "wasn't it?" Helmut looked at the grinning face with a smile and thought, If he had even the slightest inkling of my hatred, he would run away. At the same time he gave Klaus Buch a friendly pat on the shoulder and said: "Of course it was me. Weather, direction, everything that happens externally, turns into a disaster where I'm concerned. If the Israelites had had to rely on me, they would still be in Egypt."

Thank God, he had himself under control again.

While hurrying through the rain he had been thinking with disgust of the few seconds when he had been unable to hide his annoyance. There was nothing he loathed more than this state of being exposed to another person. In fact, something approaching zest for life could really only develop in him when he experienced the difference between the internal and the external. The greater the discrepancy between his true feelings and his facial expression, the greater his enjoyment. Only when he appeared to be someone else, and was someone else, did he really live. Only when he lived a double life did he live. Any directness, whether on his part or on the part of others, seemed to him unhygienic. When he gave way to an outburst—whether of anger or joy—he was usually immediately overcome by an almost uncontrollable depression. He felt at the end of his tether. Then anyone could do what they liked with him. In the apartment they could sometimes hear Dr. Zürn shouting through the house. He sounded as if about to expire from the effort required by all that shouting. Each time Helmut would think—as a kind of exorcism—Not that! Oh God, not that! He had rehearsed emergency measures against outbursts of any kind. What he had practiced was a sort of cheerfulness that may still have seemed a bit forced. This is what he now resorted to at the entrance to the restaurant.

Klaus Buch showed Helmut and Sabina the way to the restrooms. Suddenly they heard a piano being played. Quite forcefully. Klaus Buch stopped in his tracks, bringing Helmut and Sabina to a halt too. His face was working. Especially his mouth. His tongue bulged behind his lips, trying to break out somewhere, especially through the upper lip.

Sabina said: The *Wanderer Fantasy*. Klaus Buch ran outside. Helmut walked into the restaurant. Hella was sitting at the piano and playing. Sabina finally walked over to her and said something. She stopped playing. As she passed him Helmut said: "Beautiful." Sabina and Helmut followed her outside. They saw Klaus Buch dashing wildly off. Clear across the meadows. Suddenly he stopped, changed direction, ran toward a tree, leaned against the trunk, put his hands in his pockets, and stared straight ahead. Hella said: "You two go inside, we'll be with you in a minute." Then, almost too firmly and without taking her eyes off him, she walked toward Klaus.

When Helmut and Sabina came back from the restrooms, Hella and Klaus had not yet returned, but they arrived before the Halms had finished their soup. They were both smiling, walking close together, a happy couple. In their case, their soaked condition looked heroic. When they had all finished their soup, Klaus Buch wanted to know how much farther it was to the Höchste. Helmut told him they were already there. This made Klaus Buch laugh so uproariously that he had to stand up. "The Höchste!" he kept shouting. "The Höchste, Hella, would you believe it, we're on the Höchste—'the Highest'—by God, I'd call this hill the *All*-highest!"

Helmut was embarrassed by this display in front of the staff and the other guests apparently spending their vacation up here. He was also embarrassed for Klaus's sake. Helmut had the impression that Klaus wasn't nearly as amused as he pretended to be by the fact that this hill was called "the Highest." He was trying to find it more amusing than he actually did. Hella had let herself be carried away by

Klaus, but her high, ringing laughter sounded even more artificial than Klaus's.

The Halms must *please* not get them wrong, she said. For herself and Klaus, a hike was something not to be accomplished in less than six hours. To find themselves at their destination after an hour simply seemed terribly funny to them. Helmut said that in fine weather the view from here was pretty unique. When Klaus Buch was about to laugh again, Hella cried: "Klaus, please, it makes Helmut quite sad when you laugh like that."

He tried to send her a look which she would find impossible to decipher. He wished to look mysterious. And tough. And inscrutable. He knew he was not succeeding because suddenly he found himself looking only at her nose. What a nose. What an adorable little nose. He was not going to go out of his mind. When he was twenty, he had gradually come to believe: I won't go out of my mind, ever. He noticed that Sabina was aware of his profound preoccupation. He nodded to her from the depths and said: "How's the schnitzel?"

Klaus Buch swore at the food. To begin with, his schnitzel was too thickly breaded; secondly, it was pork instead of veal; thirdly, the salad was a limp mess. He did not spare the waitress. She stood there with a heavy, putty-colored face under a towering coiffure, looking miserable. When, weighed down with reproaches, she finally turned without a word and plodded off, Hella said in a low voice that the waitress's old-fashioned miniskirt was really something to behold. "A pretty unique view, I'd say!" said Klaus Buch, and burst out laughing, which made Hella follow suit. They both laughed so hard that they dropped their knives and forks on their plates. Helmut and Sabina felt no urge whatever to laugh. Sabina at least tried to put on a knowing expression. Helmut made a great effort to sound jocular as he said: "Come on, kids, behave yourselves!" Hella gave him an ecstatic look and said: "Yes, daddy." Helmut tried to continue in that vein with: "Or you'll get it," and he looked at her a shade longer than was warranted by so short a sentence.

Sabina said: "The weather's clearing up."

Before Klaus Buch, who was now obviously at the point of dissolving into laughter at the slightest provocation, could burst out again, Hella said: "Ssssh."

Helmut called the waitress and asked for the bill. The food had been excellent, he told her. It came to fifty-four marks twenty; Helmut said: "Make it sixty." He sternly rejected Klaus Buch's attempts to pay his share of the bill.

Helmut wanted to offer them some forest at least on their way back, and as soon as they left the restaurant he turned aside from the road. They entered a spacious forest. Helmut would have liked to hear someone say something about the tall tree trunks or about the green light or about the fragrant forest air.

When Otto suddenly disappeared and did not respond to Helmut's and Sabina's calls, Helene Buch stuck four fingers in her mouth and whistled so that the forest reverberated and Otto came back at once. Helmut felt that Helene Buch understood the forest. Couldn't she make it resound like that again? However, shortly before entering the forest, they had passed a wheat field, and Klaus Buch was still carrying on about the farmers, who this year, in

Baden-Württemberg alone, would be collecting 650 million marks in drought subsidies, and just look at these fields, those stands of wheat, one ear plumper than the next. Had any of them, on their way up from the lake, seen any drought damage anywhere? He hadn't. These crooks did nothing but collect. Oh well, he was just saying that because he was envious. Six hundred and fifty million marks in swindle subsidies, and not a single mark in it for him, it was enough to fill him with grief and despair. He simply couldn't see a crooked deal without being tormented by the desire to participate in it. Don't forget, he happened to be the son of a patent attorney. Really, these German farmers, said Hella Buch in a tone that emphasized rather than hid its artificiality, knew how to milk the taxpayer. On their trips through the Middle East, she and her husband had noticed time and again that there was such a thing as agriculture that could get along for years without water simply because the peasants had adjusted to producing drought-resistant crops. A Turkish peasant would never dream of trying to wangle a drought subsidy.

Helmut asked whether it wasn't demanding a bit too much of German farmers that they switch to drought-resistant crops, considering that a drought occurred only every ten or twenty years. He hoped that, in speaking these words, which unfortunately he had been unable to refrain from uttering, at least his voice had sounded pleasant. The plain fact was that he was annoyed because no one was enthusing about the forest. After all, it really was a perfect forest. And in this wetly shimmering forest this Klaus Buch was venting his spleen on drought subsidies—about which, by his own admission, he had read for the first time in the morning paper. And she ignores the forest and immediately tries to bolster her husband's obviously weak position. And he himself is still naïve enough to criticize them instead of enthusiastically agreeing with the rubbish they are spouting. Only by agreeing can you escape. Theoretically you know that. My God, how marvelous it could be now, alone with Sabina. They spoke very little when they went on a hike. At most, Sabina might put into words what they both saw anyway. She would say "a bench" when they stood beside a bench. And just when he was wondering whether the weather would hold, she would say: "I don't think we'll have any rain." And then it didn't matter one bit whether they had any rain or not because it also didn't matter one bit what one of them said or had said or ever would say. Usually he would speak up at that point and say: "Oh my love. My one and only. Sabina."

They passed through Unterhomberg. A herd of young pigs came running up across the patch they had finished grazing. Otto was convulsed with rage. The hikers, prompted by Helmut's example, pulled up some grass outside the fence to feed to the slim little pigs. The pigs crowded against the electric fencing because the hikers were not pulling up enough grass and couldn't toss it far enough over the fence. This meant that the ones in front always got electric shocks on the pink bulges of their little snouts. The pink bulges reminded Helmut of Helene's nipples.

When they were just beyond the village, they heard behind them shouts, cries, echoing hoofbeats. They immediately ran to one side. Through the village came a horse. In headlong flight. The houses looked small compared to the horse. Perhaps because it was bounding in such huge leaps. With its head held stiffly, obstinately, to one side, it came thundering out from between the houses. Its front legs rose and fell so simultaneously that they seemed to be shackled together. One man had already tried to stand in its path but, since the horse did not slow down for him, he had been forced to jump aside at the last moment. Suddenly the horse stopped. About halfway between them and the village. Two men who had been running after the horse caught up with it. One, probably the owner, reached it first, spoke soothingly to it, approached it from the front, and tried to seize it by the halter. But at that moment, just as his hand came close to its head, the horse reared and raced off again. It raced past the hikers at full tilt, farting explosively. It was all Helmut could do to restrain Otto. Probably his barking added to the horse's frenzy. It was a splendid roan with a white blaze, enormous even on the open pathway. Klaus yelled at Otto: "Shut up, you mutt!" Tossed his jacket at Hella and ran after the horse. Hella called weakly: "Don't, Klaus . . . Klaus!"

When the horse came to a halt again, some distance away, and started grazing at the edge of the meadow, Klaus slackened his speed. The closer he came to the horse, the slower he walked, approaching it in a wide arc directly from the side. Finally he was seen to grab the mane, and the next moment he was sitting astride it. The horse galloped off again. But Klaus kept his seat. A small, compact figure. As if part of the horse. Since the path turned downhill into the trees, the two were now out of sight. Meanwhile the men from the village had caught up with Helmut and the women. One of them said the kid shouldn't have done that. Now for sure the roan wouldn't give up. He would run till he was worn out. The kid would never be able to make him stop. Most likely the roan would brush the kid off somewhere.

The farmer obviously assumed that Klaus, whom he had seen only from a distance, was Helmut's and Sabina's son.

Hella had turned her back when Klaus jumped on the horse. That was how she was still standing. Sabina walked over to her. At that moment, around the bend under the trees, Klaus appeared with the roan. And when he reached them, the roan stopped. Both were sweating. Hella ran up to him. They all ran up to him. Except for Helmut. Otto was barking furiously again, so Helmut had to keep him as far away as possible. Klaus handed over the horse. The farmer said: "You could have killed yourself!" Klaus said with a laugh: "No way! He's a fine fellow. Probably just a wasp that made him bolt." The farmer shook his head, as if still disapproving of Klaus's interference. Then they parted and went their separate ways.

When they were on their own again and all expressed their admiration of Klaus, he said, putting his arm around Hella's shoulder: "You see? If I hadn't stopped that horse in Merano, I would have been scared of this one." The horse in Merano, he explained to Helmut and Sabina, had only been a Haflinger, a smaller breed. "And Hella tried to hold me back. You know, if there's something I can identify with, it's a runaway horse. That farmer made the mistake of approaching the horse from the front and talking to it. You must never stand in the path of a runaway horse. It must have the feeling that its path remains unobstructed. Besides: You can't reason with a runaway horse."

Klaus spoke with fine, sweeping gestures and great aplomb. Hella now seemed smaller than he. Helmut agreed effusively. "You're right!" he cried. "How right you are!" Sabina said: "How would you know?" "Ah," he said, "I suppose you've forgotten that I'm a horseman from way back."

It was beginning to rain again. Since Helmut could no longer promise them any sheltering forest, Klaus Buch, stripped to the waist again, ran ahead to get the car.

Helmut was walking between Hella and Sabina. Hella and Helmut: suddenly these two names seemed to him like two parts designed to be fitted together. He would call her Helene if he had something to say to her. They walked through a gang of workmen who were carrying on with their black-topping in spite of the rain. Helmut had a fleeting hope that this asphalt would only *look* like the real thing and would soon disintegrate again into slag and gravel. What he was hoping was that these men were also only producing pretense.

When they were sitting safe and sound in the car, Sabina said: "Klaus, you saved our lives." Klaus said to Hella—this time gaily, cockily, by way of parody: "You don't care for me anymore, do you." She kissed him and agreed that he had indeed saved all their lives. Helmut chimed in, and his praises of Klaus Buch were even more vociferous than the women's. Klaus was now no longer afraid of Otto's nose. Helmut could understand that.

Helmut couldn't go on listening to the others. He was about to lose the ground from under his feet. Once again he found himself forced to view his situation as a painful image. What a person sees reflects virtually nothing of what actually *is*, he thought. He saw himself lying on a rock under a cascade of water. He, Helmut, can find almost nothing to hold on to. But the deluge of water simply won't subside. The end is no longer in doubt. Nevertheless, he keeps clawing his fingers into the rock. And this, since the end is certain, merely prolongs the agony. He can clearly see himself gasping openmouthed, rolling his eyes heavenward, as in a nineteenth-century picture. As soon as he exhausted this image, he saw himself sweating and shivering. He didn't know how it was possible, but he was shivering and sweating at the same time. He couldn't have said whether he actually *was* sweating and shivering or whether he was merely imagining it to the point of physical perception.

As Sabina and Helmut were getting out of the car, Klaus thrust two paperbacks at them. One by him and the other by Hella. Helmut said it could now rain pennies from heaven as far as he was concerned, he was so eager to read these books that for the next few days he wouldn't stir out of their apartment. "You won't get rid of us that way!" said Klaus Buch. First they don't meet for twenty-three years, then Helmut wants to give them the slip right away. "Fine thing," said Klaus Buch. They would pick the Halms up at eight-thirty tonight. And tonight he would be in charge. No argument.

They drove off. Helmut ran inside, threw himself on the sofa, and stared up at the ceiling. He could have wept. Sabina pretended not to understand. He wouldn't believe her. He was glad to find

Otto frantically eager to be petted and patted by him.

On noticing that Sabina was about to say something, he jumped up and said: "I'm going under the shower for an hour."

When he emerged, Sabina showed him Klaus's book and asked if he knew that Klaus wrote his name with a *c*.

"Terrific," he said.

7 ❧ *Just before* eight-thirty, Helmut and Sabina were standing on the porch contemplating Mrs. Zürn's riotous medley of a flower garden with an absorption that Mrs. Zürn, had she suddenly appeared, would have found most gratifying. Mrs. Zürn had once told Helmut that she was embarrassed about the bars over the apartment windows, which was why she had planted phlox, foxglove, rose campion and, especially, those tall hollyhocks. Helmut had replied that once you had become used to the bars you didn't see them anymore, whereas the glorious show of flowers was a daily miracle.

He did not mention the fact that every day he noted the straight, unadorned bars at the windows with deep satisfaction. Every year, on their return to their little house in Sillenbuch, he missed the bars. Unbarred windows then seemed desolate and empty.

As soon as the car with the Starnberg license plate drove up, Helmut and Sabina hurried to the garden gate. Helmut wanted to prevent Klaus from even setting foot on Zürn soil.

Everything Klaus had recently been wearing in blue had now been switched to faded pink.

Only belt and sandals seemed to be the same.

Helene was naked and had draped something black over herself. The Buchs had reserved a table at their hotel. They were sitting right above the water. But behind glass. All the tables were occupied by little groups like theirs. The waitresses moved about. What a beautiful void, Helmut thought. Now to drink and sink to the bottom. But Klaus Buch was determined to find out whether there was any justification for his suspicion that his romantic-bizarre HH had turned into a workaholic. Helmut nodded. "Oh come on," said Klaus Buch, "I can't believe that." "Sabina," said Helmut, "what would you say?" Sabina said that Helmut worked nonstop, though in a way that wasn't apparent to everyone. He always had his nose in a book. It looked as if he were studying, but she was more inclined to regard it as living, meaning that it produced no tangible results. Maybe that wasn't even his purpose. Mind you, he did change as a result of his reading. After reading a page he wasn't the same man as the one who had turned it. Helmut gave a low whistle. Of approval. In any case, he was constantly progressing, that much she could see. At any rate, considering the tempo that Helmut had gradually set himself, she had long despaired of keeping up with him. Yes, he was welcome to give another whistle. He interjected that, although he would love to accompany her aria on sixty-four violins, all he had was two parched lips to which even Klaus would not refuse a drought subsidy. Unperturbed, Sabina said that sometimes she found his tempo pretty ruthless. He gave the impression of no longer caring whether she could keep up with him or not. Helmut said, as if he didn't mean it: "Doesn't she lie beautifully? And all the time she knows she's lying."

Klaus Buch said: "She's raving about you. Hella, why don't you rave about me for a change?"

"You take care of that yourself," said Helene.

Klaus Buch first said Hella didn't care for him anymore, then he said he was so happy to see that Helmut had not become a bourgeois.

Helmut thought: If I'm anything at all, I'm a bourgeois. And if there's anything at all I'm proud of, it's that. He decided that as a bourgeois the best thing for him to do at this moment was to smile and drink a toast to Klaus Buch, but on no account try to start discussing this designation with him. It had been a pleasure to hear Sabina talking so totally wide of the mark about his reading and living. If he imagined her saying those things when he was alone with her, all he could do was laugh. Alone with him, none of these performances would be possible. They were presentation pieces. What they expressed was a need, not a reality. She wanted to say something impressive about her husband. Perhaps she was trying to tell him something.

It turned out that Klaus Buch had asked about Helmut's attitude toward work because he liked telling people how he and Hella felt about work. They worked as little as possible, he said. "Right?" he asked. She said: "Yes, we don't need work in order to feel good." That sounded rehearsed. Klaus Buch said life was too short to waste it on work. She said, now quoting him openly and perhaps even critically (or was that wishful thinking on Helmut's part?): "Only people who are sexually inadequate need work." Now Klaus took over completely. Work was a substitute for sex. It also meant the annihilation of sex. On the other hand, sex, when taken seriously, meant the annihilation of the will to work. Anyone wanting to live must not be distracted by work. Work made a person incapable of love. Right? Or don't you care for me anymore.

She kissed him and said: "He tends to talk about it a bit too much. But that's his only fault."

"Does that mean that otherwise I'm pretty good?" he asked insatiably.

She laughed and said: "So-so."

"You admit it," he insisted stubbornly.

"Yes, I admit it," she said, laughing and kissing him.

"You're eighteen years younger than I am. Have you ever had reason to complain?" he asked relentlessly.

She put her hand over his mouth.

"I'm serious," he said.

"So am I," she said.

"You don't care for me anymore, do you," he said.

"He has to keep talking about it," she said, without having kissed her husband. "Can you understand that? I'm not that keen on this craze for verbalizing. But no doubt that's just envy because I'm not so good at it."

"You don't care for me anymore, do you," he said.

Now she kissed him. Then they both drank some of their mineral water. For the first time they seemed to be bothered by the smoke from Helmut's cigar and Sabina's cigarette. As on the previous evening, Helmut again had difficulty enjoying his wine and cigar. He drank quickly. He wanted to get drunk as quickly as possible. Should he admit to himself that he was in love with this girl Hella? What would be the point? And was it really true? Wasn't he completely indifferent to her?

Klaus Buch suddenly began to tell them about

his father's ninetieth birthday, which he and Hella had just celebrated. They had picked him up from his exclusive retirement home in Degerloch. He had been amazingly strong and amazingly feeble. But all there. Interested in everything. Name of the federal chancellor, the federal president, even the president of the federal parliament, knew them all. . . . Helmut loathed being told about old people. Incontinent, mind you, but can still reel off his multiplication tables! Probably Klaus Buch was merely anxious to demonstrate that he had another forty-five years, significant years, ahead of him. Helene said: "My mother is seventy-one and still enjoys life without restriction." Restriction, thought Helmut, with a little shudder. Trips to Africa, Persia, every year, said Helene. Nowhere, her mother had recently written, had she felt as happy as in Bali. Shouldn't it be *on* Bali? thought Helmut. "Where are your parents?"

Helmut turned his thumb straight down. Klaus said: "Show them the photos." Helene said: "The Halms won't be interested." "Go ahead, show them the photos. There's nothing more interesting than pictures of old people."

Helmut said he wouldn't like to get older than seventy.

He found this remark just as mendacious as it was true. Hence nonsensical. But wasn't everything he could say here nonsensical? Only what Hella and Klaus said really made sense. They wanted to grow old. There was every likelihood that they would grow old. They were looking forward to being able to grow old. They were doing everything in their power to grow old. They had the strength for it. Their thinking was such as to enable them to face up healthily to a ripe old age. And anyone who thought otherwise was talking nonsense. The only thing that made sense was to live to a ripe old age. A person who lives longer than someone else is more successful than the other person. The longer you outlive the other person, the greater your victory over him. Helmut wasn't sure whether that was exactly what the Buchs were trying to tell him, but that was how he interpreted the way they vied with each other in describing seventieth and ninetieth birthdays. They had celebrated by going on long drives with their respective parents. Eaten blood sausages and liverwurst on mountain meadows. Taken them to the movies. How the old folks had laughed! Look at him. And her. Just look. Poking their withered noses into bouquets. Look at that one. Sniffing up rapture from them. Just look. A continuous round of pleasures. Nothing is more beautiful than that. And the most beautiful part of all is that it never stops being beautiful till one's dying day.

Helmut said he was more grateful to the Buchs for this evening than everything else. No one, as long as he could remember, had so fortified him. So uplifted him. So richly rewarded him.

He felt his eyes filling with tears. He pretended to be embarrassed and quickly left the room. As a matter of fact, he was ready to burst into tears.

He was drunk.

Tomorrow Hella would be making her rounds of the villages, so the Halms could go sailing with Klaus. Hella would love to take Sabina along on her rounds, but she knew from experience that with two visitors the little old grannies would be twice as unapproachable. Oh, hadn't they told the Halms anything at all about Hella's new book? Klaus explains: It's going to be called: *From Grandma's Lips.* Hella drives around the villages inland, asks the mayor for the names of the five oldest women, then for the names of the three most talkative ones among them, then proceeds to drive to their homes to tape whatever good advice they can still remember. She already has thirty-seven tapes full of grandmothers. Hella says she only hopes that this book, which again is Klaus's idea, will sell better than her herb primer. "I don't know what you're talking about, my sweet," cried Klaus Buch. "Your primer is a slow burner that will feed us in the Bahamas until we're ninety years old. All right then, we'll cast off tomorrow afternoon at two-thirty." Sabina begged to be excused. She had an appointment with the hairdresser tomorrow in Meersburg. She went there every year on the same day. It was an appointment that couldn't possibly be changed. In that case, just Helmut. Klaus Buch is delighted. It'll be an orgy of reminiscing for mature men. Ciao.

Helmut and Sabina, heavy with wine, traipsed homeward. Helmut said: "Lucky you!" "My God, they're energetic!" said Sabina. "What a blessing they can't ruin more than our vacation," said Helmut. "Starnberg is too far away." Sabina took Helmut's arm and said: "Don't be so negative." "But I like being negative," said Helmut. "Are we going to have another thunderstorm tonight, Mr. Negative?" she asked pointedly. "Ask Klaus Buch, Mrs. Positive," he said. "Wicked man," she said. "I'm asking you, from now on I'll ask only you, I'll talk only to you, I'll forget every other language in the world except yours, now there!" "I was hoping that was already the case," he sighed. So he, Helmut said, had indeed progressed farther than she had, since he had long given up trying to understand anyone except her. He put his arm round Sabina and squeezed her until she squeaked a little. That made him think of Helene Buch. For the moment there was nothing he could do about that. "I'm drunk," he said. "We are," she said. "I am," he said. "We are," she said. "Who cares?" he said, running ahead of her. But she quickly caught up with him and didn't let go until they reached the apartment.

He complained once more about the way she had got out of sailing tomorrow. He couldn't understand it. She talked about this Klaus Buch like a flower in love with the wind, and then she backed out. Tomorrow wasn't her hair day at all. She was, she said with a nasty little giggle, afraid of falling in love with Klaus—whom Helmut, in spite of his promise, had again called "this." Helmut wondered whether he should rape her and throw her into the lake and prevent her from coming ashore again. "I'll forgive you this lapse and the next," he said. "I won't be offended till the third, and the one after that will be fatal, absolutely fatal." "It makes me shiver when you speak like that," she said. "That's fine," he said. "I feel warm when you shiver when I speak." "Then there will be a thunderstorm," she said. "Oh you little naturalist!" he said. "Here we are on the brink of disaster, and you talk like the weatherman. We've both been a little bit seduced at the moment," he said. "We'd better watch out. After all, we're farther along than they are," he said. "Maybe you are," she said. "Bina," he said, "I know, you aren't. Nor am I. Bina. You must resist

73

this seduction by the Buch family, my girl. Even if what they are doing is the right thing. Let's stick with the wrong thing." "Why?" she asked. "I don't know," he said. But, he went on, it had never been so important to stick with the wrong thing as now. The wrong thing is the right thing. This evening, Bina. Tonight. If they were to come together tonight, she would be thinking of Klaus and he of Helene, and the very idea of that was enough to unman him. "Idiot," she said. "Yes," he said. "Spoilsport," she said. "Yes," he said. "Moron," she said. "Yes," he said. "Asshole," she said. "That'll do," he said and, bending down to her, kissed her carefully and said: "Oh my love. My one and only. Sabina."

Only when she had fallen asleep did he breathe easily. Although it hadn't ended up as the talk he owed Sabina, they had touched places in each other that they had never touched before.

Beautiful, he thought, clothes that have been made over, how beautiful.

8 ✍ *Klaus Buch* pushed open the door for
him, Helmut got in; Klaus, in greeting Helmut, let
his hand lie a shade too long on Helmut's shoulder.
Helmut regretted that he didn't feel the same way
about this as did Klaus Buch. It would be nice if
there were someone whose hand one wouldn't
mind having a shade too long on one's shoulder.
He should have apologized for his inability to recip-
rocate emotions. Today Klaus Buch was all in white.
The blue of his eyes had never been so blue. He
pushed and pouted his mobile lips even when he
was not speaking. He was aroused. Nothing against
the women, of course, but for Fate to present them
with a day all to themselves was just great, didn't he
agree? "Man, Helmut, just us two, that's really
wild!" He stepped on the gas, then immediately
had to brake, they were already there. Klaus Buch
went into the hotel to pick up a bag. This time he
had brought some canvas sneakers along for Helmut too. Helmut doubted they would fit, but Klaus
reminded him that they had always worn the same
size shoes. Helmut had to help hoist the sails. Klaus
Buch would insist on merrily calling out each in-
struction two to four times, as if Helmut were an
idiot. Even so, Klaus Buch frequently had to come
skipping across to show Helmut where to put his
hand.

At first there were still some extended patches of moderate wind. Then the whole lake was as smooth as molten lead. Everything visible had only one color. They had emerged from Lake Überlingen and were now drifting outside, somewhere between Hagnau and Kesswil, Helmut estimated. Klaus Buch cursed Lake Constance. That it was an impotent old bag, could only do it once a day, and then so feebly as to be barely noticeable. Just look around: a landscape of muggy, floppy rags, just look, those houses over there, and those hills, just look, the sky, everything hanging, hanging, hanging, we're in for an afternoon in the Hereafter, my friend. What a shit of a lake. Frankly, if it weren't for the research to be done for Hella's book, he would never come here to sail. It might be all right for old fogies for whom the fever of life is over. Just take a look around you, this whole area, gone to its eternal rest. I swear it. Nothing happens here anymore. We are in the realm of the dead. Dreary isn't the word for it. The waters of Lethe, Helmut. Sorry. I was looking forward to a good stiff sail with you. Not a chance now. So all we can do is chew the rag. Let's chew the rag then.

He said this with incredible ferocity, his loose lips and unruly tongue moving in an obscene parody of speech. Helmut had to laugh. That put Klaus Buch in a good mood.

Christ, how they used to sail in the Aegean. They had to tie each other to the boat or they would have been washed overboard. Twelve hours at a stretch without leaving the tiller for a second. Once the boreas blew so hard that for three days they couldn't even get out of the harbor. Once they sailed from Thasos to Rhodes more under and through the waves than over the top of them. The one thing he was looking forward to was the Bahamas with their steady trade wind. Couldn't Helmut see himself joining them? Far be it from him, Klaus Buch, to wish to poke his nose into Helmut's affairs, but he had the impression that it might do Helmut good to simply clear the decks, burn his bridges, and set out for a new world. "Life needs stimulation," said Klaus Buch, "otherwise it peters out. While you're still alive. You see, it's different from ethics or morals, the world of the spirit simply exists of itself, maybe it can generate its own tension, I really don't know about that, you're the expert there. On the other hand, *I* know that living matter needs an impetus. In fact, what living matter needs is the totally new. Nothing can be new enough for it. The newer, the more alive. The totally unpredictable reaction, if you follow me, that's life. Tell me, Helmut, how often do you screw your wife?"

Helmut must have given him such a look that Klaus Buch did not insist on an answer. "Or to put it another way," he said. "Are you quite sure you still love your wife? Please, don't misunderstand me, Sabina is really a wild woman, I envy you Sabina, but even the wildest woman can be a threat to men of our age. If she doesn't have it anymore. Hella could also be a threat to me. If she didn't have it anymore. But she still has it. And how. Hella is a challenge for me. She's too much for me. I can't cope with her. It's a constant struggle. Day and night. It keeps you in shape, that's for sure.

"After you've been in bed for a month, you can't

 77

walk half a mile, that's how far gone your muscles are. It's like that with *everything,* Helmut. I'm truly fascinated by life, Helmut, believe me. When a raindrop splashes onto my skin, I could scream with delight. When I look up into a tree, I could shriek for love of chlorophyll. But I'm scared of my mind going to seed, Helmut. The danger exists, I know that. I'd like to stay brilliant, you know? Bright. Outstanding. And noble. Noble through and through. Like untearable silk, that's what I'd like to be. Raw silk, of course. I am a worshiper of myself. To some extent Hella also worships me. Because she considers me more intelligent than I am, you know. I go on pretending to her. I keep her smaller than she is. I persuade her to do things that are beyond her. Just in case I can't cope with her, you know. What I really need is a person like you, Helmut. I mean it. When I saw you sitting there on the promenade, *ecco,* it was a vision. My old HH, forever gnawing away at problems, reading *Zarathustra* in his swim trunks—Helmut, if you come along to the Bahamas, it'll be the salvation of both of us. There you can do anything you like in your swim trunks. What would you be giving up here? What school are you at anyway?"

"Eberhard Ludwig," Helmut said, doing his best not to sound proud.

"Oh," said Klaus Buch, "congratulations—oh well, you were always tops, of course. Even so I make so bold—imagine, me, old cockroach, never been anything, never become anything—I make so bold as to offer you—a Ph.D. and revered teacher at illustrious E.L.—some far-reaching propositions. I maintain that it's necessary. You need to be saved. You need me, Helmut, I can sense that. Hence my question, how often do you screw Sabina? I don't mean to humiliate you, man. I'm not trying to make like the Body Beautiful. Christ, Helmut, toward the end I used to screw my first wife only once a week. That's the kind of shape I was in. *We* were in. So there. Feel free to talk to me. If you want to. I simply feel that, before we reach fifty, we two should launch out again. And without you I am in danger of mental stagnation. I'm quite aware of that. You are truly a challenge for me. You and Hella, then things will start to hum. No problem."

Helmut nodded as often as he could. Klaus Buch must be under the impression that Helmut was seriously considering these propositions. That stimulated him to even further suggestions. Since Helmut had not yet shown any readiness to speak, Klaus Buch said, he could only continue to bare his soul in an effort to provoke Helmut into abandoning his reserve—a reserve so threatening to himself —so that they could at last jointly pursue their joint salvation. Helmut was—and he, Klaus Buch, felt this quite clearly—acutely aware of the danger of stagnation. Maybe Helmut had even resigned himself to it. But he, Klaus Buch, didn't think so. He was more inclined to think that Helmut was temporarily playing at resignation but that, as soon as he realized that it was no longer a game, he would try desperately to escape from that resignation. Then it really would be too late. Or at best a panic action. But there was still time for them to plan their second launching together. And in such a way that it would succeed. Without anybody getting hurt. That was the crucial point. He could say that the separation from his first wife had come to pass without either of them getting seriously hurt. Precisely because he hadn't waited for panic to set in. So, as far as he was concerned, the offer was unconditional. He suspected that Helmut might already be suffering the first damage inflicted by the unappealing routine of finality. *Might* be! he had said. And his offer, far from being prompted by compassion, was downright selfish. The more Helmut made use of him, the more emboldened he would be to make use of Helmut. And, after all, they were such old friends that they could be quite ruthless about offering mutual assistance. No inhibition must come between them. Helmut could consult Klaus Buch if he wanted to know how he could split up with Sabina with a minimum of damage—provided that was what Helmut wanted, of course, he was only mentioning it as an example because every man who still has life in him wants to split up with his wife, only the dead are faithful. But Helmut would be just as welcome to consult him if in need of reassurance as to the length of his penis; this, too, he was merely mentioning because every man who still had life in him was interested in any chance to test his own competence. If for once two men were to join forces they would carry off a tremendous victory. If each of them remained alone, each would have to wangle his own miserable way through life, seizing loot, securing loot, consuming loot, seizing more loot, and so on. "Helmut, man, let's aim for the top. Not settle for less. Remain great. Become greater. The greatest. We two are the greatest, I swear it. Life is calling us. I'll get you out of your doldrums, kiddo. I'll fix you up again. You'll see, in a year you won't know yourself. You're on the point of going under. I refuse to watch. I'll turn you on, man. I'll put such an appetite into your belly, you'll go straight up in the air, want to bet? First off, you'll come to us in Starnberg. Just for a few days. That'll get the whole thing rolling. And it'll just keep rolling, I'm convinced of it. Helmut, man, in Starnberg, you know, I often sit naked on the terrace from four to seven in the morning, listening to the birds. There's no sound in the world like it. I have some huge trees in my garden, that's where the birds start up even before the sun has properly risen. But not first one and then the other: like in an orchestra, all the ones which belong together start up at the same time. Some come in gently, some clamorously. And the next moment a positively inconceivable number of birds are singing. But you don't see a single one. So the trees themselves seem to produce the sound. And you can no longer tell that this chorus comes from individual birds. It might just as well be coming from a giant pipe organ. Or from a few hundred organs being played on their highest registers. And it doesn't sound in the least like outdoors, more like an echo chamber. Like a giant echo chamber resounding, reverberating, with birds' voices. It's as if the whole world were reduced to the nave of a church. And the fantastic part is that the chamber itself, the nave, just imagine, doesn't stay in one place, it rises, you can hear it, it rises up into the air. But it doesn't budge an inch. That's the most staggering part. It hovers. It really does. It hovers. In the air. The chamber just keeps on growing. And echoing. A vast chamber consisting of nothing but birds' voices. A bird-cathedral, formed by a reverberating multitonal sound. My dear Helmut, that's when I have to go indoors, but on tiptoe, as silently as the first ray of sunshine; and although I'm in the mood to shout and stamp, to leap in the air, dive onto her, no, I snuggle up to her and caress her awake, but even before she is quite awake I have the seduction already in place so that, when she opens her eyes, when her lips part, she already desires me. Capito?"

A squall hit the boat and with a resounding crack blew the sail to the other side.

"Hello there, we have a visitor!" cried Klaus Buch, grasping the lines and the tiller.

Helmut had not been able to look very long at Klaus Buch's mouth either bulging out or split open by a tongue run riot. He had fully understood the haste with which Klaus Buch had been speaking. While Klaus Buch had been talking as if for dear life, Helmut had kept his eyes quietly on the surface of the lake, the surface of the sky, the gradually materializing shoreline. Almost imperceptibly, colors had reappeared. In the sky, inky patches of every shade of blue had flowed together. In the course of the afternoon, everything had grown more definite. At some places in the inky streams there were now even distinct silvery borders. Only the western sky still consisted of an endless transparency. A real pink. Helmut was reminded of "the real thing." The water had absorbed all these colors and concentrated them in a dense blend. In the water one could see all the blues, the silver, the pink; together they produced a blue of increasing steeliness flooded by a violet gold. And it was into this that the thundery squalls ripped their black scars.

"Storm warning!" cried Klaus Buch, letting his tongue break through his mouth and pointing enthusiastically across to Switzerland and back to the German shore. At many places, yellow warning lights were flashing. A color otherwise not present. The squalls came from all sides. Klaus Buch swore. "It's gone crazy!" he shouted. He meant the wind, he said. He looked around belligerently, not to be caught napping by the approaching squalls. "We need headway, then the squalls can't hurt us," he cried. Squalls with no wind, he had never seen such a thing. Helmut was to tend the jib sheet. When Klaus Buch called *let run,* he was to pay out the line but never let go entirely; when Klaus Buch called *haul in,* he was to take in the line. While he was still speaking, a gust passed over them that Klaus answered with a leap to Helmut's side. "Boy oh boy, was that ever a handful!" he cried. He explained what Helmut had to do when they came about. Helmut asked whether they were now heading for the German or the Swiss shore. For the time being they would be sashaying with these totally crazy squalls, said Klaus Buch. As soon as those were followed by a wind from one direction, something that was to be expected even on Lake Constance, they would carry on with their afternoon sail. Helmut pointed to the storm warnings. He was afraid. Among the darkened colors, the many glaring lights flashing away at various points looked ominous. Klaus Buch pointed to the darkest part of the sky: an advancing thunderstorm, that would give them just what they needed. Helmut said he would rather they tried to reach land as quickly as possible. Switzerland seemed closer to him. Why not make for Utwil or Kesswil and phone Hella from there, maybe she could pick them up with the car? "And us at the roadside with the sail under our arms, right?" Klaus Buch laughed. Helmut said they could also wait out the storm ashore. Probably the German side was easier to reach after all, since the wind was coming from the southwest.

Klaus Buch said it was high time for Helmut to stop evading life. Another squall hit them, Klaus Buch called out: "Let run!" But Helmut let go too late. Since Klaus Buch had luffed the mainsail in time and compensated with the rudder, they survived the squall nicely. But it was immediately followed by the next. Helmut shouted: "Klaus, we'll have to head for shore!"

By now the lake had turned into a light green, whitely hissing surface. Klaus Buch shrieked with delight. Helmut thought, Maybe he really is crazy. Klaus shouted to Helmut to sit on the side of the boat. Helmut moved up. They were now racing full tilt toward Switzerland. Theirs was the only boat left on the lake. Close to the shore they could see boats without sails making for the harbors, probably with their engines.

Klaus Buch behaved more and more like a rodeo rider. He talked to the wind. Gave every approaching squall a new name. "That's Susie, trying to crush us between her thighs, attaboy, let run! There she goes!" Each time they righted themselves after a gust, he would give Helmut a happy laugh, pat the hull, and shout: "Good girl, *Seabird*, good girl!"

Helmut saw that it was becoming increasingly difficult to cope with the wind pressure by maneuvering and shifting ballast. Flying spray had long since soaked them to the skin. He was holding his jib sheet by the very end. "Haul in!" roared Klaus Buch. Helmut shouted: "You're nuts!" He was convinced the boat would capsize as soon as any strain was put on the jib. The wind was producing a sharp, machine-gun rattle with the flapping jib. "Full warning!" Klaus Buch shouted triumphantly. True enough, the lights were flashing twice as fast. "Head in now!" yelled Helmut. Klaus Buch shouted: "Coward!" Helmut couldn't take the excessive heeling of the boat anymore. The waves were already washing aboard. So this Klaus Buch was a madman after all. By leaning their weight as far out as possible and keeping the sheets completely slack, they now managed to hold the boat on the very verge of capsizing. But the storm increased. The boat began to heel still farther. Helmut simply let go his sheet. The snapping and rattling became ominous, as if someone were hammering away at them. Klaus Buch shouted: "To make you happy, we'll re-eef!" He turned the boat straight into the wind. The boat righted itself immediately. Thank God. Helmut could breathe again. Klaus Buch called out: "Get over to the tiller! Hold it between your legs! Keep the boat heading straight into the wind! Don't be such a sissy, man! Grab ahold of it! As if it were part of you!" He laughed and skipped over to the mast. Helmut had no idea how, in the midst of all the roaring and snapping and rattling, he was supposed to achieve anything with this ridiculous piece of wood. It seemed like midnight to him. Suddenly he felt a pressure on the tiller. The boat was no longer heading straight into the wind. He jerked. But in the wrong direction. The mainsail swung clear across. Klaus Buch yelled something. Rushed at Helmut, grabbed the tiller out of his hand, bent down for the lines. Helmut felt sure the boat was about to capsize. Certainly it would if Klaus Buch hauled in the mainsail again and the boat was once more at that appalling angle. When

Klaus straightened up, working with the tiller and the sheets to bring the boat under control and the boat started to heel over again, Helmut shouted: "Don't!" Klaus Buch shouted back: "We're taking off!" And laughed. Preposterously. And hung terrifyingly far out over the side of the boat. He was practically lying on his back. The boat had resumed its appalling angle. It was obviously going to capsize within the next few seconds. "Come along, sweetheart," Klaus Buch yelled. "I need your weight!" Helmut positioned himself on the hull but kept most of his weight inside the cockpit. Now Klaus Buch was even tipping his head back as he shouted, *Lucy in the sky!*" When Helmut saw that the waves washing aboard were about to pour into the cockpit, he kicked the tiller out of Klaus Buch's hand. Then everything happened at once. The boat shot back into the wind. Klaus Buch toppled backward into the water. The boat righted itself. The wind caught it from the other side. Helmut ducked just in time as the mainsail whipped across. Then he cowered beside the mast and looked around for Klaus Buch. The instant before Klaus hit the water, Helmut had received one look from him. The mainsail had torn loose. Mainsail and jib were flapping before the wind, which was now coming from behind. In spite of the rattling of the sails, it was suddenly much quieter. Helmut cautiously got to his feet, his eyes scanning the white crests and the dark troughs. "Klaus!" he shouted. Louder and louder: "Klaus! Klaus!" When he realized that he was now only shouting for his own benefit, he stopped. Be quiet, he thought. Don't try anything now. Just keep quiet. Klaus should be able to take care of himself. A sportsman like him. If they should ever capsize, Klaus had lectured, the thing to do was let yourself be carried by the waves. Never try to reach a nearby shore against the waves. It was absolutely no problem to swim three miles *with* the waves, but impossible to swim five hundred yards against them. Absolutely no problem. So there. Idiot. Forget about it. You didn't mean it to happen! You *didn't!* So there. Then why are you on the defensive? You didn't mean it to happen. Finish. Klaus can look after himself. But you can't. That's the way it is. He would cling to this boat. If it sank, he would go down with it. But maybe it wouldn't sink. Klaus Buch had said something about buoyancy tanks. He looked around for places to hang onto. He refused to look out of the boat. But to judge by the snapping and rattling he must still be making headway. By now it was almost dark. It was raining. Klaus.... Oh Sabina, if you only knew. Had he ever felt so utterly shattered? He gave a great wail. During those last few months, when he had still been having sex with Sabina, he had experienced exactly the same sensation, that of being destroyed. Each time it was as if he had committed an irremediable error. Each time he had wailed like that. A long-drawn-out, steadily rising wail. His life was only to be endured, he had felt, if he continued, and never ceased, to emit those high-pitched, infinitely prolonged, muted screams. But he wasn't allowed to. Each time this happened, Sabina was so alarmed that he had to break off at once. He had told her he only did it for fun: she could see for herself, his eyes were completely dry, he enjoyed uttering these little cries. But Sabina had said, if that were so she didn't want to live, those sounds were so terrible.

Now he was free to scream as high and long as he wanted. Once again he had committed an irremediable error.

Only when the keel suddenly scraped the gravel along the shore did he stop crying out. He jumped into the water, waded ashore, and headed for the nearest light.

The people were alarmed. They called for an ambulance. They urged him to drink tea laced with brandy. He was in Immenstaad, they told him. They notified the water police so that action could be taken immediately to rescue his friend. They telephoned Sabina. They telephoned Helene Buch. Helmut thought he had better remain apathetic. In Unterhomberg Klaus had said you couldn't reason with a runaway horse. He had agreed.

9 ✒ *Helmut stood* at the window, looking through his binoculars at the foxglove blossoms where the ants, ten times their real size, were crawling over the aphids and milking them. "Voyeur," said Sabina. "Shouldn't you phone Helene Buch?" he said. "If she hasn't heard anything by now, she won't hear anything," said Sabina. "Have you noticed, the red lily opened up during the night?" he said. "I'm sure she would call us if she'd heard anything," said Sabina.

Helmut walked up and down on the Kirman rug. "Why don't you call her," he said, "just to be on the safe side?"

Sabina got up and, reluctantly, went over to the Zürns'. It was all right for her to do that. In all the eleven years he had never used the Zürns' telephone.

Once when he had been walking around on this pale Kirman with the dark blue medallion, he had been obsessed with the notion that clutching his right hand was a person the size of a seven-year-old child, and that this person was Friedrich Nietzsche, aged forty but reduced to the dimensions of a seven-year-old. And his terrible fear of Otto made him cling to Helmut's hand.

Klaus Buch had later had exactly the same fear of Otto as Helmut had observed in his miniature Nietzsche.

Helmut was in the habit, when walking up and down on the Kirman rug, all alone, of talking unconsciously to himself. "Quiet," he would say, "quiet, quiet." And after a certain interval: "All the dead, move up one; all the dead, move up one."

It was a very old habit, this *Quiet,* and *All the dead, move up one.* As soon as Sabina had left the room he now said: "Quiet, quiet," and, after a pause: "All the dead, move up one; all the dead, move up one." But he had a feeling that today he had started to speak not automatically but consciously.

Sabina reported that Hella still had no news. "Aren't we going down to the lake at all today?" he asked. She couldn't bear the sight of the lake today, she replied. Mrs. Zürn had told her that, according to the newspaper, three people had been drowned in yesterday's storm. One had drowned although two motorboats had reached the capsized sailboat and thrown ropes to the yachtsman, who had been clinging to the hull. The waves had torn him away from the boat and, unable to reach the ropes, he had disappeared before the very eyes of his rescuers. Helmut nodded as if he knew what it was like. Sabina put her hands around him and nestled against him. Helmut responded as far as he was able. He would go down to the lake anyway. Maybe she would come later. "How did Hella sound on the phone?" he asked. Her voice had been very low and miserable; she had hardly said anything. Just yes and no. Helmut picked up the first volume of Kierkegaard, quickly left the house, and walked down toward the water. Otto was happy and scampered along with him. They were greeted outside by the Zürns' spaniel Florian, who always wanted to start something with Otto. But Otto, a bitch, invariably fought off the advances of Florian, a male dog of the same age, as fiercely as possible.

Today the lake presented itself as rimless. Serene. And innocent. Helmut liked that. In that softly blue, shining, rimless expanse, not a soul would have recognized the hissing monster of yesterday. A haze, in itself invisible, made everything visible look blue, indirect, mild, insubstantial, airborne. No limits anywhere. No contrasts. Only blending. Wasn't this a day when one might apply the word *endless*? Might have, if . . . He could feel his heels. Ice-cold. As if lying in snow. All night long he had kept putting his hands around his heels and been surprised each time to find that they felt quite normal. The moment he released them, though, they signaled a pain which he perceived as icy cold. The first time he had had this feeling was on their first sailing trip. . . . That's right, just carry on. Last night, when they had finally driven him home and all he had wanted was to get into bed as quickly as possible, a huge insect had lain on the mat by his side of the bed. A beautiful green grasshopper. Helmut had almost stepped on it. He tried to pick it up but, in its death throes no doubt, it had fastened its claws into the fabric of the mat.

He had to use a little force to pull it off. One of the two long antennae was drooping. Otherwise the beautiful green creature was completely intact. Its hemispherical eyes apparently could not be closed. Helmut had thought: Carry on. Wings like a tailcoat, he had thought. A green neck-plate like a Regency collar. Or like Klaus Buch's golden, collar-length shield of hair. Suddenly the creature had drawn up the long lower half of one hind leg and then let go again. Then the whole hind leg had started to twitch. It was actually jerking back and forth. The other hind leg was twitching a little too. The long belly was quivering. He couldn't bear to watch. He placed the little green, horselike creature on the windowsill between the iron bars, crawled under the quilt, and tried to make himself tremble. He actually did. For quite a while. But then he had to yell at Sabina. Her whimpering made everything that much worse, he shouted. Whereupon Sabina wailed without restraint. But after that she quieted down. By morning the grasshopper was gone.

He opened his black Kierkegaard book and began to read: *During my sojourn here in Gilleleie I visited Esrum, Fredensborg, Frederikvaerk, and Tidsvilde. The latter is known chiefly for St. Helen's Spring, to which the entire local population makes a pilgrimage on Midsummer Day.* Helmut shut the book. He did not know how to face the situation.

Suddenly he felt that from now on ceaseless attacks were to be expected from all sides. Not a single innocuous minute was left.

Suddenly everything was unpredictable. He couldn't go on lying here. One thing was certain: reading was the least feasible activity. He had to move. He should. If he could. Oh God, don't lose your mind the very first day, one can cope with much worse things, self-defense, my God, self-defense. You didn't mean it to happen. If he'd carried on with his crazy rodeo we would have capsized. And neither of us would have survived. It's in the paper, isn't it, stop-stop-stop, you mustn't think like that, go ahead, admit it, let your conscience safely graze, what does that mean, I ask you, to let your conscience graze, must be a contest in verbal prostitution, stop, admit, you can't cope with it, your memory serves you as never before, no trace of charnel house. Intense is the word, you actually *lived* in that instant, you went out of yourself, HH, for an instant you failed to maintain your pretense, this is the instant you are stuck with, will be stuck with, when the rupture of that instant can no longer be closed.

He stood up, ran back to the house, and said he wanted to go for a jog through the forest with Sabina. Sabina was taken aback. A nice easy one. No athletic ordeal. Just a suggestion of a long-distance run. "Long-distance run, Sabina, d'you know the expression? I love it. Long-distance run. Just start off very gently. Running shoes. We've no running shoes. Look, I'll make a quick trip into town and get us some running shoes, track suits, running shorts, running shirts. Please, don't laugh, don't cry, it's all so meaningless, we have to get moving. If you don't want to swim, we'll run instead. Let's behave like opportunists. Come on, Sabina, jogging for the masses. D'you want to come into town with me? We can borrow a couple of bikes. From the Zürns. Would you do that? Please, please, Sabina, do go and ask them if they can lend us two bikes, no wait a minute, we'll buy some, yes, at last things are starting to hum"—too late, the Klaus Buch expression had slipped out, and Sabina had recognized it as such—"we'll buy two bicycles, across from the Löwe, the shiniest bikes they have, then we'll ride into town, buy our outfits, and ride into the forest, then we'll park the bikes and go for a jog. Let's go."

Sabina had to be pushed. She tried to nod. She was probably thinking of Klaus Buch. But she did not say his name. They walked into the village and bought the best available bicycles. In town they bought their outfits. Then they bicycled back along the lake road to the apartment. The cycling was fun right away. They were less awkward than they had feared. Helmut said: "Oh Sabina, am I glad we thought of bicycling! That's the right way to begin. How easy it is. A real success situation, don't you agree?" "Yes!" Sabina cried. "Just wait," he cried, "once we've changed our clothes it'll be even better." He felt that nothing could stop him now.

Back in the apartment they changed with undiminished haste. By now Sabina had been infected by Helmut's urgency. They both moved effortlessly. They decided they looked funny in their track suits, but not ridiculous. In fact, she looked most intriguing, said Helmut. Like a woman athlete from one of the trans-Ural Soviet republics. "You," she said, "look like a top American executive on a Saturday." He was a bit worried, though, that he might have bought his running shoes a size too small. "At last I recognize you," she said. But he would tolerate no delay.

Just as they were reaching for their bicycles, up drove the old silver Mercedes. It was Helene Buch. She wasn't in the least surprised to see the Halms holding bicycles and wearing track suits. She herself was dressed in a way that the Halms had never seen.

Ancient, patched jeans, and a navy blue, double-breasted pinstripe jacket over a T-shirt that had once been black. And her hair close to her head. Now it could be seen that her neck was almost curved. Now it could be seen that she needed this lovely long, gently curving neck to lift that gentlest of little noses high into the air.

She hadn't been able to stand it another minute in the hotel room, she told them.

The Halms put away their bicycles and went indoors with Helene. Sabina made some coffee and asked Hella what she would like. Hella said she'd be happy to join them in a cup of coffee. Sabina said with a query in her voice that she also had some homemade cherry cake. "Yes, I'd love some," said Hella. They each had two pieces of the cake. Hella said it was the first piece of cake she had eaten in four years. It was the best she had ever eaten. A cup of coffee and a piece of cake, what could be better, said Helmut. Without them, he said, life wouldn't be worth living. He hoped Hella and Sabina realized that he was spouting all this nonsense just so the silence wouldn't be unbearably prolonged. As soon as no one had anything more to say, this cake-eating became a repulsive ritual.

Sabina then cautiously asked whether Hella would mind if she smoked a cigarette. "No, of course not," said Helene, smiling a bit like a convalescent. She felt she could use a cigarette today too. Sabina offered her one.

The most remarkable sight now was Helene smoking. She inhaled deeply, tranquilly. Like a person making very sure.

At one point she said: "I'm intruding. It would be nice, you know, if you could behave as if I weren't intruding. If, for instance, you were to read now, I'd know I wasn't intruding. I just don't want to be alone, not right now."

Sabina asked if she should make another pot of

95

coffee. Helene nodded with gentle eagerness. "We could also offer you a twelve-year-old Calvados," Sabina said. Helmut frowned and said brusquely: "Sabina!" They were to do whatever they would normally be doing, said Helene, otherwise she couldn't stay here another second. Sabina was welcome to put down a glass of Calvados beside her, then she would feel less of an intruder. Sabina poured a Calvados for each of them. Helmut said: "Not for me." Helene said: "Why aren't you smoking?" Helmut waved away the idea. "I like it when you smoke a cigar. My father used to smoke cigars too."

While they were sitting there, Sabina and Helene drinking their coffee and Calvados and smoking, Helmut said: "I don't know, Sabina, would it be better if I talked about what happened, or would it be better for us not to discuss it now? I simply don't know. Hella, you must tell me what is ... more acceptable to you, it's up to you." Helene looked up. He had actually said "Hella." Perhaps for the first time. Instead of answering, she started weeping convulsively. A loud, long-drawn-out wail. Helmut sprang to his feet and paced up and down, his steps jerky and angry-looking. Helene also stood up, forced him to stop. Then she started weeping again, this time leaning her head against him. He could feel the sobs shaking her. He led her back to her chair. Sabina was wailing too. Helmut could not prevent his own eyes from filling with tears. Suddenly he remembered Sabina having said she couldn't go sailing because she had a hairdresser's appointment. Helene must have noticed long ago that Sabina hadn't been to the hairdresser.

Helene drank the Calvados that Helmut had refused. Sabina filled all three glasses again. Helene was the first to reach for the refilled glass.

"Do please smoke your cigar," she said. "I'm quite sure you would be smoking now if I weren't here."

Sabina also gave him an encouraging nod. Helmut said: "No, really. Not at the moment. Maybe later." Helene, again ostentatiously, placed a third glass of Calvados in front of Helmut, then raised her own glass to him. He shook his head. She and Sabina drank. Helene said: "God, this Calvados is good! Six years ago I spent a semester studying at Montpellier, and I used to drink Calvados quite often. With thick, thick walls all around." Helmut could not help thinking of the thin walls of the hotel at Grado. He looked across at Sabina and saw that she was thinking the same thing. That annoyed him. "Montpellier," said Helene, "was the most beautiful time in my life." This statement sounded funny.

She finished her drink. Sabina poured her another. "Now I'm the only one drinking," she said.

"Cheers," said Sabina and drank too.

"I'm leaving tomorrow morning," said Helene.

"For Starnberg," said Sabina.

Helene nodded.

Helmut had a feeling he would never be able to move again. And that he would ever speak again also seemed unlikely to him.

"Klaus," she said, half to herself, "would probably say that life must go on."

Obviously she was on the verge of tears again. Obviously this time she would fight them. She bit her lip.

"It's just that I don't know how," she said.

She continued to fight back more mounting sobs. She finished her glass. Sabina filled it.

"Klaus once told me," she said, " 'You only have to care for me as long as I'm alive.' And now I have a feeling I'll never be able to believe he's dead. I can never get that into me. Never. For me he's still alive."

She drank up her Calvados and held out her glass for Sabina to fill. "Cheers," she said. Sabina drank too.

"He didn't have much of a life," Hella said. "It was just one long grind. Every day ten, twelve hours at the typewriter. Even when he couldn't write, he still sat at the typewriter. 'I must be at the ready,' he would say then. Everything he did was a terrible effort. That's why he tried to give everyone the impression that he didn't work at all, and that whatever he did was for the sheer pleasure of it, effortlessly. Yes, without effort, he wanted to seem to do everything without effort. And then always the feeling that whatever he was doing was a fraud.

"That one day he'd be caught out. He often used to cry out, at night. And more and more often he would break out into a sweat, in the middle of the night. That's why he kept saying: 'We'll clear out to the Bahamas.' When we were alone he used to add: 'And join the other crooks.' He was absolutely convinced that he was a crook. Needless to say, we didn't have the slightest prospect of moving to the Bahamas. We could hardly afford even this kind of a vacation here. Even in the hotel room, he kept on working every day. And I was supposed to collect grandmothers' sayings. That's over now. That's the one thing I'm sure of. Never again, as long as I live, will I touch another tape. Never again a typewriter. I couldn't tell him how little that appealed to me, forcing my way into quiet villages, asking the mayor, interviewing those dear old women, explaining how and why and what a microphone is. But he was so thrilled with his idea. He was a child. Or wanted to be a child. 'A person can do anything.' That was another of his sayings. He should have become an athletics instructor. Or an explorer. But not in this day and age. A hundred years ago. Captain of a sailing ship. Adventurer. Someone who surmounts every obstacle. As long as it's caused by Nature. In the face of Nature he was always courageous, ingenious, invincible. Only with people ..."

She made a plunging gesture.

"He was fantastic with his hands. The cottage in Starnberg was a chicken coop when we bought it. A refugee had wanted to start a chicken farm and didn't make it. Klaus did it all himself. And how. A terrace, you've never seen anything like it. Of red sandstone. That red terrace is his monument. It will survive, I know that. But actually he was finished. I mean it. He was in the wrong boat. And he forced me into that wrong boat too. That's how I know what it's like to be in the wrong boat. It's hell. By some idiotic chance he got into this lousy journalism. And on top of that into this environment stuff. Then he believed he had to take the whole thing seriously because it's our bread and butter. He was so uptight about it. Toward the end he had rows with everybody. And I do mean everybody. He hated the editors and publishers' readers he depended on just *because* he depended on them. If one of them showed the slightest trace of criticism,

Klaus would tear up his own manuscript before their very eyes. That was really wild. Ridiculous too, of course. He always had a copy. Everyone knew that. He was just waiting for them to stop him. They would just grin."

She finished her drink, held out her glass, had it filled, said "Cheers," and drank. Sabina drank too.

"And the way he insulted people he depended on, that was really wild. Just because he depended on them. And his publisher, the way he bugged him. For a while he drove regularly into Munich, and what he used to do to that publisher's car. . . . I'd hate to tell you. He really was finished. Totally and utterly finished. That's why he was so happy that we bumped into you. 'Now we'll make a go of it,' he said after our first evening. He was a fantasist. Right away he started about the Bahamas again. Off to the Bahamas with Helmut. That was his latest idea. Life with him wasn't that easy, I can assure you. Because he was so touchy. Because they let him feel they didn't need him. Once they had let him feel that, it was all over. That's when he began, a hundred times a day, I swear, a hundred times a day he'd ask if I still cared for him. He saw himself more and more as the lowest form of dirt. And it was my job to keep proving to him that he wasn't the lowest form of dirt but a supersupersuperman. And convincingly, too. I mean it."

She jumped up. Walked up and down. Holding the glass. Having it filled. Drinking.

"It had become practically impossible to talk to him. Gradually I was coming to realize I wouldn't be able to stand it much longer. More and more I felt as if I had to hold a drowning man above water. When I could no longer do it, he would drag us both down. I realized I wouldn't be able to go on doing it forever. That's why I was equally happy we bumped into you. You see, we were totally isolated. Totally. Please, don't get me wrong. You know I don't want to say anything against Klaus. . . . I want . . . I just have to say . . . I must tell you . . . I must tell someone, how . . . I am . . . I was hardly . . . if I could say this just once. . . . I wasn't allowed to live, he didn't permit it. I had to show far greater interest in what he was doing than he did himself. As if I had been his daughter: what he couldn't achieve, *I* was supposed to achieve. I was his pride and joy. On the other hand, he resented it when someone praised something I had done. He was crazy. Because he realized that no one needed him, he had reached a level of egotism that can only be called pathological. I was studying music when he met me. From one day to the next I had to give that up. We'd known each other for less than three months when he decreed that I would never make it as a real musician—give it up, you'll only make yourself miserable. Basta. There. Then he started indoctrinating me with his interests. I was twenty-two. And a fool. I was such a fool, you know, the Matterhorn is nothing by comparison, that's how great a fool I was. Of course I also know he can't help it . . . but why me . . . why should I be the one to pay? I had to sell my piano. Believe it or not! He developed a fanatical hatred for music. It was either him or music! One more year, and I would probably have succumbed. Then I could have stood it forever. Cheers. Isn't it amazing, the things people can put up with! I have him to thank for that. I've learned that once and for all. I can stand a lot. I . . . d'you want to bet that I can stand more than the two of you together? Come on, let's have a bet. I'd like to win. It's so long since I won anything. I feel I . . . you've no piano here in your fancy apartment. Not even a violin. What a lousy deal. A vacation apartment with no piano. And no violin. And for eleven years. Eleven years with no piano or violin. You can put up with a lot. You must be pretty hardened by now. Let me feel, Helmut. Are you hardened? Your soul? Let me feel. Your earlobe. Don't you know? Like earlobe, like soul. Hm, you have a rather flabby earlobe, I would say. And you, Sabina dear? The fact is, women do have fuller earlobes than men, you find that over and over again. And talking of women, mmm! I tell you, there are some women with such fullness, you can forget about men. What is a man, Sabina? Full of hot air, okay. What else? Nothing. Klaus had . . . ah Klaus . . . Somehow I seem to be floating in a liquid. And I'm also drinking some of the liquid I'm floating in. I must say, it really is a bit out of this world. If only it doesn't suddenly come to an end. Helmut, you'll see to it that the phone doesn't ring all of a sudden—Mr. Stahlhagen calling from Munich to say he won't be wanting anything more from us. . . . I'll be forever in your debt for all you two have done for me, I mean it. You really are the greatest. And by the time we meet up with you it's practically too late. What rotten luck. Helmut, you can't imagine how happy Klaus was to have run into you. 'It's like finding buried treasure,' he said. You—he felt that—you with your quiet, determined manner could have made him whole again. That's what he lacked, your common sense, your sense of proportion, your inner calm. Oh you two dear things, you can give me a little bath now if you like. I'm staying here with you. And you'll give me a bath. With a big sponge. You don't have a bathtub? You just have a shower, like us. A bit on the skimpy side, wouldn't you say? Never mind. Would've been rather nice if you had given me a bath. But that's the way it is. I, creature of luxury that I am, would like to get into a tub. But there isn't any tub. Just like in the Sahara Desert. There's just a chance I might get sad now. But please, don't take it to heart. A hot bath is the best thing for sadness. It must be good and hot. When I'm lying in a hot bath I always start singing. Although otherwise I haven't been singing at all recently. I tell you, it faded away so quickly, my singing. To practically nothing. Sometimes I sit there exuding silence. And there I sit, in that silence. Like under a glass cover. Then, ladies and gentlemen, it gets to me. *It* gets to me. Depression, I mean, the resentful, self-devouring kind. Because now I'm worth no more than something you throw at the wall to smash it so completely that you can't tell from the pieces what it was or what it was meant to be. That's really the most important part, for the destruction to be thorough enough. If they were to only partially smash us all, there would be a wave of sympathy in which we'd all be sure to drown, and that would be the end of the world. But as people who have been smashed to smithereens we go on living without feeling. I thank you.

"And now, without further ado, we'll start. We've already wasted too much time. Ladies and gentlemen, as an artist I am not as well prepared as I would like to be. But in a different way I am much too well prepared. So I take the liberty of asking for your attention. I shall now play for you the *Wanderer Fantasy* by Franz Schubert."

She played the notes in the air, sang the notes, punched out the rhythms, drew lines with her fingers. She walked up and down, stopped, turned around. She performed the piano piece as if reciting a text. She didn't omit a single syllable and explained exactly how she meant it.

There was a knock. Helmut ran to the door. Mrs. Zürn. A gentleman had come to pick up his wife.

Past her, past Helmut, Klaus Buch walked into the apartment.

Helmut gave Mrs. Zürn a quick nod, then closed the door, ordered Otto to heel, and kept his eyes on the dog.

"Klaus!" screamed Sabina.

Helene, abruptly breaking off her music, said, as if wilting, expiring: "My Klaus, my dear, dear Klaus. There, what've I been saying all along? He's alive, I said, and what is he? Alive. And how late he is! That's just like him. He simply wanted to know what we do when he's not around. Right? You devil. Didn't I tell you he was a devil? Klaus, do find yourself a comfortable chair, I just have to finish playing the *Wanderer Fantasy.*"

She found her place and resumed. But not for long. She looked at Klaus and, keeping her eyes on him, poured herself a Calvados and said "Cheers," then drank it down and looked at Klaus again.

Klaus said: "Come along now."

She said: "Didn't you like it? Forgive me, there you stand, freshly rescued, and I'm playing the piano: it wouldn't surprise me if you were to classify me as an egoist. You who have been snatched from the waves. He always triumphs over Nature. I told them that in advance, didn't I?"

Klaus said: "Come along now."

Helene said: "But Klaus, do let's stay with our friends for a while. There's no bathtub in our room anyway. They don't have one here either. So we might just as well stay here. Either way, we'll play out our fate of being without a bathtub. No problem."

"I'm leaving now," said Klaus.

"Has someone upset you?" she asked. "I can see, you're offended. Klaus, quick, tell your Hella who offended you. Whoever it was, I can see he really hurt your feelings. I can see that. Eeeeh! They've really, really hurt our Klaus's feelings. I'll put new life into you, lover boy, and before very long too. I swear."

She lit another cigarette, took Helmut's straw hat from its hook, and put it on. "May I borrow it?" she asked. And then she said: "Let's go, genius, onward and upward."

Waving to Helmut and Sabina, she went out the door, somehow taking Klaus with her. All the time he was there, Klaus Buch's and Helmut's eyes had not met. Helmut realized this now. So he was to preserve the look in the eyes of the man toppling backward. Klaus had probably seen through him at that moment as no one had ever seen through him before. And the man who had seen through him like that was alive. They did not move until they heard the car driving away.

Sabina said: "Hold everything."

Helmut sat down, lit a cigar, poured himself a

Calvados, and said: "Cheers." And drank. Sabina did not drink. "Do you know what got into him?" Sabina asked. Helmut ignored the question. "Helmut, what's got into him?" asked Sabina. "Something's the matter. Instead of wanting to celebrate, he arrives . . . like Doomsday personified. Can you explain that?"

Helmut picked up his black Kierkegaard book and said: "If you're looking for your Wagner—*My Life*, it's over there, shall I get it for you?" Then he opened his Kierkegaard book and read: *During my sojourn here in Gilleleie I visited Esrum, Fredensborg, Frederikvaerk, and Tidsvilde. The latter is known chiefly for St. Helen's Spring, to which the entire local population makes a pilgrimage on Midsummer Day.*

He closed the book again. Sabina had not stirred. "Come on," she said. "We wanted to go for a bike ride, remember? Into the forest. A jog through the forest. Let's go." Helmut stood up and said: "I can't wear these things." He started to change. While changing, he told Sabina they could give the bicycles to the Zürns. They would simply leave them behind; they could always use them again if they ever came back here for a vacation.

He said: "Please, Sabina, you change too. Please."

He spoke again in that firm, compelling voice with which he had insisted on buying the sports outfits.

When they had both changed, he said: "What would you say if we started packing now? Or maybe: I'll pack, you find Mrs. Zürn, pay her for the four weeks, and whatever you do, don't accept a reduction, say something about special circumstances and if we come back next year we'll let them know in good time, and so on. Please, please, Sabina. I'll tell you all about it when we're on the train. Please."

Sabina sat down and said all this was much too fast for her. In a withering, utterly convincing tone of sheer blackmail, he said: "Then I'll have to go alone." "Is that so?" said Sabina. "But I'd like to make a speech, too," she said. "When do I get to make my speech, if you don't mind? Perhaps you think I'm not entitled to make a speech, is that it?"

"Oh Sabina. My one and only. Sabina," he said.

"Don't," she said.

"You're right," he said. "On the train, Sabina, on the train."

He began to pack. Gradually she joined in. When she was on her way to the Zürns, he called after her: "A taxi, in fifteen minutes." Trim Mrs. Zürn and two of her tall daughters stood at the door waving as Helmut, Sabina, and Otto drove off. Dr. Zürn, fortunately, was away in the Algäu. At the ticket counter Helmut said: "Two and a half, one way to Merano." "Merano," said Sabina, shaking her head. "Why Merano?" "Just a moment," said Helmut to the clerk, "my wife doesn't agree. Where else then?" Helmut asked. "To . . . to Montpellier," Sabina said, exhausted. "Two and a half to Montpellier, one way, first-class," said Helmut. "I hope you won't find it too hot there," said Helmut. "If the walls are that thick?" said Sabina with a little grin.

Helmut kissed Sabina carefully on the forehead. Otto made a sound as if he were suffering. Sabina gave Helmut a look that made him say: "You're looking right through me as if I were an empty jam jar. Wait a bit. On the train." Sabina said: "Last night in my dream I was supposed to know the word for a number that is not divisible by any other, and I didn't know the answer. Everyone else did. Including you. But even you wouldn't help me." He ruffled her hair a bit contritely. The train was arriving. Helmut said to the locomotive, which was brown with a white stripe and reminded him of a father confessor: *"Qui tollis peccata mundi."*

When they had found a compartment to themselves, he said: "Sabina, now we don't have to move till we get to Basel."

Sabina said: "I'm a bit scared about the heat after all. What will we do if it's too hot down there?"

"Oh," said Helmut with a shrug, "sew shadows together."

For a while they sat across from each other silently, like strangers. She facing the engine. He with his back to it.

"What really happened yesterday?" she said.

An express train rasped by.

"It's rather a long story," he said, looking out onto the Rhine. "The Rhine," she said. She stretched a little. She was sitting in the evening sun. He in the shade. He intensified his voice as never before and said: "Oh Sabina. My one and only. Sabina." He could see that she liked the sound of it. This encouraged him to soar to heights that he felt bordered on hyperbole.

"Suffused in light, my Sabina," he said, "with your strength of which you are all unaware. Looking out from the years as from a bower of roses, that's what you're like."

"Very nice. And now?"

"Now I'll start," he said. "I'm sorry," he said, "but it's just possible that I'll be telling you all about this fellow Helmut, this woman Sabina."

"Go ahead," she said. "I don't believe I'll believe all you say."

"That would be the solution," he said. "So, here goes," he said. "It was like this: Suddenly Sabina pushed her way out of the tide of tourists surging along the promenade and headed for a little table that was still unoccupied."

About the Author

Martin Walser was born in Wasserburg, Germany, in 1927. He is perhaps best known both here and abroad for his novel *Marriage in Philippsburg* which won the prestigious Herman Hesse prize and was translated by New Directions Press. His ten novels and many plays have consistently won both critical and popular acclaim in Germany where his works have often been on the best-seller lists for months at a time. He has lectured widely in the United States, and taught at the University of Virginia, the University of Texas, and Dartmouth. He now resides in Überlingen, Germany.